The Dragons of Kilve

One day the dragons of Kilve have a wonderful surprise. Some ancient dragon eggs—which had long been forgotten about—begin to hatch, and Horace, Maurice, Clarys, Sparky and Treasure are born.

The unexpected arrival of the baby dragons turns the peaceful life of the dragons of Kilve upside down. It leads to all sorts of adventures and mishaps: Igneous and Furnace get into a hot spot, Maurice's pride leads to a muddy fall, and Treasure lives up to her name.

The wise old Dragon Master is always close at hand to comfort, cheer and encourage the sometimes wayward dragons. And, best of all, he helps them to discover three great secrets...

Beth Webb lives in Somerset with her husband and four children. She illustrates books for adults with learning disabilities and her first children's novel, *The Magic in the Pool of Making*, is also published by Lion Publishing.

For Gabriel and Gabrielle who
first told me about the dragons

The Dragons of Kilve

Beth Webb

Illustrations by
Jenny Press

A LION BOOK

Published by
Lion Publishing plc
Sandy Lane West, Oxford, England
ISBN 0 7459 2747 5
Albatross Books Pty Ltd
PO Box 320, Sutherland, NSW 2232, Australia
ISBN 0 7324 0777 X

First edition 1993

Acknowledgments
My thanks to Gabriel and Maddy
for helping to think up the stories.
Also to John, Tom, Laurie and Peter.
Why not?

A catalogue record for this book is available
from the British Library

Printed and bound in Great Britain
by Cox & Wyman Ltd, Reading

Contents

Maurice, Clarys and Horace
carried Treasure this way
←

Igneous and
Furnace played here

'Beautifulling'
Mud

Kilve
Bay

FOREST

Golden Dragon's
lair

MIDNIGHT

The Dawn of Time

Long before you or I could remember, when the world was still young, there were many strange and wonderful creatures unlike anything you have ever seen. They were the stuff of dreams and legends.

There was the great serpent Leviathan, peering with baleful, hungry eyes through the endless dark of the deepest seas. She was so long, she entwined her cold, luminous scales three times around the middle of the world.

The dreaded Behemoth, huge and hideous, haunted the molten depths of the boiling earth, guarding its deadliest secrets.

The tiny, nasty-minded Rehab hid under slimy stones and dreamed dreams of havoc.

Wild, white, untamed unicorns cantered across the green open fields, flinging their milky manes into the burning sunlight. Freedom and wind were the blood of their veins.

High in the air, above them all, rose flights of dragons, some gold, some red, others purple and pink. And in a rocky bay not far from here lived the mischievous blue-green dragons of Kilve.

The Creator gave all these beasts friends, a Master or a Mistress, to help them when the world became too difficult or strange.

The Master of the dragons of Kilve was every bit as exciting and wonderful as his creatures. He was as old as time, with wild white hair, and a long hooked nose. His piercing eyes always took the colour of the sea, whatever the weather. Draped in his deep blue cloak of stars, the Dragon Master wandered ceaselessly about the earth, watching and caring for his silver-winged friends.

1
Horrible Horace

The dragons of Kilve had long green heads and silver wings. Their eyes were huge rubies, and their claws gleaming daggers. When they flew high in the bright blue, sun-filled skies, their shining scales glimmered and glinted in the light.

They spent their days circling high among the clouds, and diving deep into the clear, turquoise seas for fish.

In the evenings they would stretch out on the cool stony shore, and talk and sing with the Dragon Master as he told wonderful stories. Then they would spin yarns of feats of flight, laugh at jokes, and scratch each other's scales. Sometimes, they would walk with him along the cliff tops and watch as the golden sun slipped silently into the slate-grey evening sea.

If they were sad, the Dragon Master always understood. If they were hurt, he would make them feel better. Then, as night fell, the Dragon Master would pull his dark blue cloak of stars over his beloved dragons, and they would sleep.

One day the dragons had a wonderful surprise. A dragon egg, which had been laid many hundreds of years before and forgotten about, had hatched. A small, green-blue dragon crawled out from the leathery little shell, shook his thin, transparent wings and yawned.

The other dragons were so pleased, they spent all day pampering the baby, whom they called Horace.

Whatever Horace wanted, he had. Flamethrower built him a beautiful little rocky nest at the back of a cave. But Horace did not like *that* cave, so Flamethrower had to move the nest to another one.

Igneous spent all day catching the fattest fish because Horace was always hungry. But he would eat only cod, so the older dragons were left with the mackerel, which was really far too indigestible for them.

Others brought treasures from their own hoards for the baby to play with. Ember brought a deep red ribbon from a real mermaid's hair, and a mauve crystal to hang in the cave to catch the light.

Fireworks did coloured smoke displays for

Horace, and Fizzle the deaf old dragon smuggled him chocolate biscuits when Ember wasn't looking.

Everyone adored Horace. After all, he was their only baby! Meanwhile he grew fatter and greedier.

One day he was lying on his back, sunning his tummy, when suddenly he pointed a long silver claw up towards the sky.

'Want!' he demanded. 'Gimme!'

'What, dear?' asked Ember.

'Ball!'

'I can't see a ball, dear.'

'*That* ball. Gimme!'

She looked up. Horace was pointing to the sun.

'That's not a ball, dear, that's the sun,' Ember said kindly.

'Want!' screamed the baby dragon, and he stamped until the rocks started to fall.

At that, all the dragons came down from the heights of the sky, and out of the depths of the sea. Horace's screams were so terrible, the dragons were certain that some monster was trying to kill their precious baby.

Horace would *not* cheer up. He screamed and howled for the rest of the day and then the whole night as well. No one had any time for the Dragon Master, so he pulled his cloak of stars over them all, and hoped they would get some sleep.

Day after day, things got worse. The baby dragon grew thin and pale, and his scales began to drop—he wanted the golden ball so much!

At last the dragons could stand no more. They could not bear to see their only baby so ill, and they were quite worn out.

They were too tired to walk with the Dragon Master at the day's end. They forgot to laugh together. They were sad, and their aches and pains were never made better.

Everyone was very unhappy.

So, leaving Pumice, the old wingless dragon, to look after baby Horace, all the other dragons spiralled up into the bright blue sky together. Between them they carried a huge bag. They were going to catch the sun.

Up and up they flew, but soon they became very tired. They couldn't breathe. Their wings and claws ached, and they dropped the bag. One by one they fell away, spinning and twisting back down to the sea.

Wet and exhausted, they crawled into their caves and slept. They did not even notice the Dragon Master when he came that night. He shook his head sadly, pulled his deep blue cloak over them, and let the stars shine out.

Next day, the dragons decided that instead of

flying *up* to get the sun, they would wait until evening, and catch it as it sank *down* into the sea.

So they flew to the Midnight Forest and spent all day searching for the tallest tree. Then they stripped the branches to make a long pole. Then they wove a seaweed net and tied it to one end. They were going fishing for the sun!

As evening approached, they set off towards the sunset. Now dragons can fly extremely far and fast, but however hard they flew, the sun was always just ahead of them. At long last, it slipped silently into the sea, and disappeared.

The dragons kept on flying until they reached land, and there they slept. Next day, they cheered as the sun rose. Perhaps, if they flew high into the sky and waited, they could catch the sun as it came towards them!

But the sun climbed higher and higher—too high for them to fly. Soon it was straight overhead. Then it went past and beyond them. The dragons could never catch it before it fell into the sea again!

On and on, all night they flew, beating the air with their weary, silver wings, looking for somewhere to land.

Suddenly, just about dawn, Flamethrower pointed a claw below. 'Look!' he roared, 'there are hills ahead ... and ... it's Kilve!'

'Don't be silly!' scoffed the others. 'We've flown for two days over land and sea. We must be thousands of miles away!'

'Then we've gone in a circle!' he groaned, gliding in a steep spiral down to the rocky beach below. One by one all the other dragons landed next to him. And there they stayed in exhausted heaps until the Dragon Master found them.

'I've been so worried about you. Why didn't you let me help you?' he asked sadly, as he stroked their throbbing backs.

The dragons hung their heads.

'But what could you have done to help?' asked Ember, easing a weary wing back into shape. 'Could you have caught the sun?'

'You never know until you ask,' the Dragon Master chuckled. 'Bring me a big bucket of water, and your bad baby dragon.'

So they did.

The Dragon Master had a little talk with Horace about not whining for things he couldn't have, then they gave each other an 'I still love you' hug.

'Now look,' said the Dragon Master . . . and in the top of the bucket shone the sun!

'Ball!' squeaked the baby dragon delightedly, splattering the surface of the water. Then he started to cry loudly. 'Ball broken!' he wailed.

'Just wait,' said the Dragon Master.

The water stilled, and Horace clapped his wings with delight. 'Ball back!' he giggled.

'Now,' said the Dragon Master, 'you can play that game as long as the sun is high. But when you can no longer see the sun in the bucket, you'll know it is time to come and look for me.'

'But what happens if we need you when the sun's still in the bucket?' asked Ember, who was always very concerned that everything be done the proper way.

The Dragon Master laughed and gave a loving scratch to Ember's gleaming blue-green scales. He pointed to the glittering sun in the bucket. 'I'm here now, aren't I? I'm never far away, especially if you really need me.'

2
Fire Games

Not everyone was thrilled at Horace's arrival.

Two particularly lazy young dragons called Igneous and Furnace soon got fed up with fetching and carrying for a rude and demanding little baby, so they ran away to the other side of the Midnight Forest. And there they stayed, playing hide-and-seek, sunbathing and making up silly songs. The Midnight Forest was a lovely place to be. It was so cool and dark—as dark as midnight in some places—very different from Kilve, where everything was sea, rocks or sky. Here Igneous and Furnace could hide in the cool darkness and have fun on their own. They were very pleased with themselves.

But after a while, they became bored and lonely, so they had fire-breathing competitions. At first they burned down only dead old trees, but soon that became too easy. So they tried to burn the greenest, dampest trees they could find. Then they tried to blacken whole copses in one breath. Not to be outdone by each other, they chose bigger and bigger targets for their furious fires. Soon whole stretches to the west of the Midnight Forest lay ruined and hundreds of animals and birds were frightened and homeless.

Far away, on the rocky, northward shores of Kilve, the Dragon Master knew what was happening: but how could Igneous and Furnace be stopped? The Dragon Master could summon terrible fires to blast the two dragons to cinders—but that would only make *him* as bad as *they* were.

Closing his eyes, the Dragon Master thought. Igneous and Furnace had to *want* to stop being so terrible. If only the West Wind would blow . . .

That night, when he had tucked the other dragons up in their caves, the Dragon Master left the cool shores of Kilve and went to visit young Igneous and Furnace in the forest.

From a long way off, he could hear the cries of the terrified creatures whose homes had been ruined or burned. The sounds broke his heart.

First, the Dragon Master tried to reason with the dragons, but they were so bad that they pretended they couldn't hear him. Soon, they found they really *didn't* hear him. They had learned to 'unlisten'.

Next, a brave lion came to the Dragon Master and begged to be allowed to try to talk to the dragons. 'After all,' said the lion, 'I am the king of the beasts. They must obey me!'

The Dragon Master wasn't at all sure, but he said 'yes,' and watched. Sad to say, the dragons did *not* listen, although they *were* pleased to see the lion.

They had him for supper.

Then, a wily old snake called Stanley told the Dragon Master that he and his friends had a plan to make the dragons stop their fire games.

The Dragon Master did not want to let them, because of what had happened to the lion. But the snakes insisted that all would be well.

That night Igneous and Furnace were sleeping after a really big blaze which had taken all their puff. When the dragons began to snore really loudly, the snakes moved in. Very slowly and silently, they tied their long, thin bodies in tight, scaly knots around the dragons' feet.

Then, without a stir of wind, the owls flew overhead, and hung on the dragons' wings. (As you know, if a dragon cannot flap its wings, it cannot take a really big breath, and without a really big breath, it cannot blow fire.)

The two dragons woke suddenly, howling in pain because owls have very sharp claws. But the brave creatures hung on.

For two whole days and nights, they clung onto the fearsome, wriggling beasts. At last, hungry and exhausted, Igneous and Furnace gave in.

'We'll do anything you say,' moaned the bad dragons. 'Only let go of us, *please.*'

The owls dug their claws in harder and the snakes tightened their coils one more turn. The dragons howled in pain. 'Ow! Leggo! Stoppit! Pleeese!' they wept.

'Now lisssten,' hissed the snakes. 'We will hang onto you for ever—if you don't ssstop your wicked fire gamesss...'

'We promise! We promise!' howled Igneous.

'And you-hoo will go-o far away from the Midnight Forest for ever?' demanded the owls.

'Yes! Anything!' sobbed Furnace.

But, sad to say, as soon as the snakes and owls let go, the two terrible dragons burst out laughing. And they laughed until they cried, sending boiling streams of tears down their red-hot noses.

They rolled onto their backs and snorted and spluttered and giggled fit to burst. Their scales all stuck up on end, and they lay helpless in the charcoal dust.

'Ho, ho! What a joke!' squealed Furnace.

'This really is too funny!' howled Igneous, until the ground shook as they thrashed about with their long tails. Nervously, all the forest animals peered between the blackened tree stumps to see what was going on.

At last Stanley, the snake who had led the brave crew, slithered over to Furnace.

'*What* is so funny?' he demanded.

'It's . . . It . . . it's juuuust . . . Oh hoo hoooo! My tummy aches!'

Igneous rolled over on the blackened ground and broke a few more animals' homes. 'It's just . . . we don't give . . . a . . . oh ho, oh no . . . !' and they started laughing again.

With a supreme effort, Igneous fixed Stanley with one dark red, glinting eye. 'It's just we don't give a fig for promises. We kept our claws crossed, so we don't have to do what we said!' And then he started roaring and snorting all over again. Then to prove the point, the bad dragon blew a burning yellow plume of fire into the sky . . . before eating the brave old snake.

The Dragon Master was furious. He itched to do something *really* nasty to the terrible pair, but he knew it would be wrong. He had to think of something else . . .

But he did not have to think for long.

Igneous and Furnace spent the whole night rolling around in helpless laughter, throwing flames everywhere, making the midnight sky bright orange with fire. They did not notice the damage their fire was doing. All around them the ground was becoming too hot, even for dragons. By morning, their feet and wings were badly singed, and they were very unhappy.

The Dragon Master felt very sorry for them. He asked if they needed any help, but they turned their backs him and pretended he wasn't there.

They felt very cross and sorry for themselves.

The Dragon Master waited.

The next day, with injured wings and sore feet, the two dragons tried to drag themeselves to water, for even fire breathers need to drink. But they found their flames had dried all the lakes and rivers for miles around. Then they saw big black clouds sailing overhead, so they lay on their backs with their mouths open, miserably waiting for rain. But there were no trees left to help the clouds to drop their water, and the rain never came.

And so it went on. Day after day, the dragons grew thinner and thinner, hungrier and thirstier, and more and more sorry for themselves. They felt alone and very sad.

After a while the Dragon Master came and stood in front of them. Igneous and Furnace *wanted* to see him now, but they were very ashamed, and tried to hide their heads under their burned wings.

'I have a suggestion,' said the Dragon Master quietly.

'Yes?' Igneous and Furnace pricked up their ears hopefully.

'I suggest that you follow me,' he said. And he turned and walked away.

Mile after mile, he led them. They followed on painful feet, dragging their useless wings, but not daring to disobey. All around them was blackened forest and emptiness. They felt so ashamed. There was nothing to eat, and nothing to drink, and it was all their own fault. They felt *dreadful*.

At long last, when Igneous and Furnace felt they could not crawl another step, they stopped. Below, in a rocky, blackened valley, they saw—water.

The two thirsty dragons scrambled down the fire-scorched rocks to the pool below, and they drank and they drank until it was dry.

When they had finished, the Dragon Master spoke quietly again. 'If you crawl down into the caves at the bottom of this valley, you could use your dragon fire to mend things. You could blast some new underground water channels and divert streams back to the burned forest. Without water, the land will never recover.'

'Why should we?' snapped Furnace.

Igneous sat down and pushed out his bottom lip.

The Dragon Master just shrugged and turned to go. 'It was just an idea, but it's up to you,' he said.

After sitting alone by the empty waterhole for another two days, the dragons realized they were in real trouble. They were weak and hungry, their wings were too burned to fly and the little pool had not filled up again.

'Come on,' said Furnace miserably. 'Let's find these underground caves.'

Igneous nodded. 'You're right. We made this desert, and if we don't do something we'll be stuck here for ever.'

No one saw them again for a very long time, but here and there, new springs appeared in odd places along the floor of the old burned forest. Eventually, small plants and even little trees began to grow. Life was returning.

At last Igneous and Furnace crept out of the caves. When they were sure there was plenty of water and that new plants were growing well, the young dragons began to make their way back towards Kilve.

But when they reached the last great hilltop

which looks down on the whole of that wild and rocky coastline, the two lonely dragons hung their heads. They couldn't possibly be wanted at Kilve any more.

Igneous sat down heavily and curled his long green and blue tail around his feet. 'I . . . I don't want to go back just yet. Let's stay here for a bit. No one need know we're here. We can just *look* at Kilve for a bit . . . perhaps we could go down in a few days . . .?'

'I feel the same,' said Furnace. 'I want to go back, but I can't.'

There was a long silence. 'Do you think the Dragon Master might help us?' Furnace added doubtfully.

Igneous shrugged. 'I don't see why he should,' he replied sadly. Then he put his long, thin green head on one side and looked wistfully down at Kilve. 'But you know, Furnace, I think he *will* help us—one day.'

3
Treasure

One night, Igneous and Furnace were walking along the edge of the Midnight Forest, looking down at Kilve. They wished they could go back home, but they were still worried that the others would not want them back.

Suddenly, they almost trod on a twitching little leathery bundle.

By the pale starlight, they could see it was a dragon egg about to hatch. A tiny silver claw appeared, pulling at the leathery shell. Then another. Then a whole arm and a leg, a pointed head and a long, thin little body slithered out of its broken prison. A tiny baby dragon lay panting on the grass.

'It looks a bit odd,' said Igneous.

'It's just the dark,' said Furnace. 'It'll be all right by daylight.'

So they fed the baby dragon some caterpillars and curled up next to it to keep it warm until dawn.

But when morning came, they had a shock, for the little girl dragon had no wings.

'UGH! Tread on it quick!' screamed Furnace.

Igneous felt all sick and cold at the sight of her. He wanted to squash her too. He could say they'd rolled on her by accident while they were asleep . . . But the Dragon Master would know it was a lie.

'No,' he said, firmly. '*All* dragons are precious. And this one needs help quickly. Perhaps the Dragon Master can do something. Who knows? We must take her to Kilve.'

Furnace shuddered. He didn't want to go back, and he did not want to touch the pathetic little wriggling 'thing' that lay on the grass in front of them.

'*You* can go. I'm staying here. I'm not going to risk my neck for . . . *that!*'

'Well, just help me get started, will you?' said Igneous as he peered up into the trees for an empty bird's nest. At last he found what he wanted and put it down next to the tiny, helpless baby.

'In you hop,' he said kindly. But the little thing was too weak. So, very gingerly, he hooked her in with one claw.

'It'll be dead before you get home. It's not worth

the effort,' said Furnace sulkily.

'*She* will be fine, if only you'll help. Put the nest up between my wings so I can carry her home. Then you can go back to the Forest, if that's what you want.'

Furnace wrinkled up his nose and held the nest with his claw tips, as if the little thing had some terrible infection. He settled the nest between his friend's wings. But it was not easy. It kept slipping.

'Walk with me a bit of the way and hold the nest, Furnace, just until we get to the edge of Kilve. If she falls from my back it will kill her.'

Furnace muttered something horrid, but did as he was asked.

As the odd little procession swayed its way down the cliff paths to the bay, Furnace and Igneous felt very scared. 'What if they throw rocks at us? The Dragon Master is bound to have told them what we did to the Midnight Forest,' said Furnace.

Igneous was worried too. 'Perhaps we should wait until nightfall, then we could sneak in and leave her at Ember's cave—or even with Pumice?'

Furnace peered into the nest on Igneous' back. 'She looks very weak. I don't think she'll last that long unless she gets help. We've *got* to keep going.' Furnace felt himself blushing. He'd forgotten he was the one who had wanted to tread on the baby only an hour before. 'Besides,' he blustered, '*you* couldn't "sneak" anywhere. When you're being "quiet" you make enough noise to scare Leviathan herself!'

As it happened, Furnace and Igneous need not have worried about their reception at Kilve. The place was alive with noise and bustle, and their arrival was ignored.

The day before, Horace had been playing football with Fireworks and Fizzle when the 'ball' had started to twitch! They had been using *another* dragon egg! After a long search, they had found several more long-forgotten eggs. Pumice immediately took them all into her cave for safe-keeping, 'Because I never play football with my visitors!' she told everyone crustily.

Early that morning, two of the eggs had hatched.

There was a lovely long, thin girl dragon they called Clarys, and a short, fat boy dragon they called Maurice. The arrival of these two caused such a stir, no one had time to be cross with Igneous and Furnace.

When they tried to show Ember their find, she brushed them aside and said she was very busy and would they *please* keep out of her way.

Flamethrower bustled past and told the two young dragons to make themselves useful. Igneous tried to say, 'Please, Flamethrower, we need your help,' but the dragon's long green-blue tail had already disappeared into the next cave.

Everyone they spoke to was in a hurry. It was hopeless. How could they get help for this sad, wingless baby dragon that no one had even bothered to name?

Miserable and dejected, Igneous and Furnace sat on a rock next to the sea and looked at the nest and its tiny occupant, wondering what to do.

'I'm hungry!' announced Furnace suddenly, and he launched himself into the skies. He soon returned with two fat cod—one for himself and one for Igneous—and a sprat or two for the baby. The big dragons began to enjoy their lunch, but the baby dragon just gave a tiny shake and stared at the sprat. Furnace, with his mouth full of cod, said, 'C'mon 'ittle 'un—s'good for 'oo.' But she still didn't eat.

'Don't talk with your mouth full!' grumbled Igneous. 'It's a bad example for the baby. I think she's too weak to eat,' he added, breaking off a tiny piece of fish and with one claw he gently opened the baby's mouth and pushed the food inside. She swallowed and blinked one garnet eye.

'She's taken it! Give her another bit, quick!' squealed Furnace delightedly.

Just then a gravelly voice behind them said,

'What *are* you two young ruffians up to?' It was Pumice. That meant *trouble*.

The two dragons crawled aside and let the ancient wingless dragoness peer into the nest.

'And *when* did she arrive?' Pumice demanded, peering at the young dragons with a fierce gaze.

'P-p-p-please, P-P-Pumice ... we found her up on the hillside, late last night. She's poorly, and she needs help, but everyone's so busy with the other hatchlings, no one wanted to know about her ... She's broken you see, she's ... she's ...' stammered Furnace, staring guiltily at where Pumice's wings had once been.

'I can *see* exactly what's wrong with her, you young idiot!' roared Pumice. 'Don't just stand there gawping, fetch me whelks and winkles, mussels, anything tiny! And you, the stupid-looking one,' she shook an imperious claw at Igneous, 'Warm me a puddle of water if you haven't forgotten how to breathe fire.'

Igneous and Furnace winced at that, but Pumice took no notice. She was too busy roaring orders. 'Fetch the Dragon Master. *MOVE!*' And with a twitch of her scaly old tail, she swept the nest, baby and all, into her cave and disappeared.

Igneous and Furnace wasted no time. One always obeyed Pumice immediately.

By evening, the little dragon was looking much greener and fatter as she sat next to Pumice by the fire in the Great Dragon Circle.

First, the Dragon Master called Maurice and Clarys forward, and older dragons named them in front of all the others. There were cheers, and much rattling of wings. Everyone was very excited. But when the wingless one wriggled forward, there was an embarrassed silence. The other dragons looked away, or tried to persuade Horace that it was bedtime. 'Who is going to name this dragoness?' asked the Dragon Master. There was silence again.

'Go on, you two, you found her!' ordered Pumice with a painfully sharp poke of a claw into Igneous' ribs.

Igneous found himself standing next to the little one. Her big garnet eyes glinted and looked up at him with love.

'I name her Treasure. She's the best Treasure a dragon ever had!' he proclaimed loudly.

This time there *were* cheers, although not many.

Suddenly, a voice from the back yelled, 'But we're not going to *keep* her, are we? I mean, the great Pumice excepted, what *use* is a wingless dragon?'

This time there were murmurs of agreement from some of the dragons. The others stayed silent, waiting to hear what the Dragon Master would say.

The Dragon Master looked at Igneous and Furnace.

'Well?' he said simply.

Furnace wriggled up to the fire and stood the other side of Treasure. Eyes blazing, he peered round the circle of huge green-and-blue dragons. 'Of *course* we're keeping her. Every dragon is precious, even broken ones!'

'But what *use* is she?' the voice came again. It was Fawkes, a quarrelsome and unpleasant dragon. 'We'll have to spend all our time looking after her. She'll always be slowing the rest of us down from what we want to do. I mean, she'll always be a problem, won't she?'

Igneous could feel his fire rising in fury. But he said quietly and firmly: 'If it wasn't for her, we would still be out there all lonely in the Midnight Forest. She gave us a reason and the courage to come back and say we're sorry to everyone.'

Furnace's green and blue scales were bristling with anger. 'And *I* never realized before that it's *nice* to do something for someone else. I say she stays. She's *our* dragon. The West Wind must have blown her to us, and with us she stays until she is blown away again... And what's more... we love her...'

For a few seconds Furnace hesitated. Then he

drew a deep breath and added quietly, 'And ... *I'm* sorry for burning the Forest too.'

Quietly, the Dragon Master gave the two dragons a proud and pleased hug, as everyone (except Fawkes and one or two others) cheered and roared and rattled their wings until the rocks began to fall.

4
Dragon Flight

As the baby dragons began to grow up, it became obvious that Horace was in for a shock.

Maurice did not like playing football and he *hated* getting into mischief. All Maurice cared about was trying to get his unruly scales to lie flat and admiring his reflection in rockpools. He never liked flying more than was necessary because it ruffled his wings and dulled their luminous glow.

The lady dragons had a shock too. Clarys took no notice of them whatsoever. She *loved* football, and spent her days seeing how high she could fly and how fast she could dive into the great wild waves. In the evenings she and Horace would crawl through the wet and filthy tunnels behind the caves so they could bounce out suddenly behind unsuspecting dragons and scare them half to death.

Pumice was shocked as well, but for a different reason. No one, apart from Igneous and Furnace, was the least bit concerned about Treasure. So, old and frail as she was, Pumice kept Treasure in her own cave and looked after her. Igneous and Furnace did what they could, of course, but sometimes they were more of a well-meaning hindrance than a help!

Day after day, the four little dragons grew long and sleek. Their ruby eyes glinted in the sunlight, and their silver dagger claws grew sharp and strong. Horace, Maurice and Clarys soon took their turns in fishing the wild seas with the other dragons, but Treasure stayed quietly next to Pumice, learning about the seaweeds, and the meals and medicines that could be made from them. She learned which rocks, ground into powder, could be used to treat wing-rot, and how to listen to the voices of the wind and sea to hear what secrets they told about the weather. Soon she knew when the wind would be calm and when the storms would be too wild for even the bravest dragons to fly.

Treasure learned well. She spent long hours with her turquoise tail wrapped carefully around her, so the rougher dragons would not accidentally-on-purpose tread on it when they passed her. Quietly she watched everything that happened at Kilve, until she began to understand things the other dragons missed completely.

The Dragon Master spent much time talking with Treasure, which made Horace, Maurice and Clarys jealous: not that *they* could be bothered to stop and talk to him. One day, when the Dragon Master had given Treasure a pretty pink stone on a chain to wear, they decided the time had come to act.

'Look, there she goes,' muttered Clarys between her teeth, 'she thinks she's *so* special, pink crystal and all. Dragon Master's pet, *that's* what she is! It's not *fair!*' Clarys knew she was being silly. She never wore jewels of any sort. They got in the way when she was crawling in the deep underground caves.

Horace said he hated the way that Treasure was always right about everything. 'She always knows when it's going to rain. She can tell when the cod are shoaling, and she can *smell* when the wind is going to change. You're right, it's *not* fair.'

Maurice was smoothing his wayward scales. '*Treasure's* scales always lie quite flat and shiny... I wish she wasn't here at all,' he added quietly.

The others looked at him. A gleam came into Horace's eyes, and a nasty smile hovered at the corner of Clarys' mouth.

That afternoon, the sea breezes were gentle and the sky was a lovely deep blue. Clarys brought

Treasure some fish. She had a lovely smile on her face, but her fangs showed just a little. 'We've been thinking, *dear* Treasure, that it can't be fun, never flying, so Maurice, Horace and I are going to take you for a *little* flight—wouldn't that be nice?'

Treasure tried to say, 'Thank you, but I'm not really worried about not flying, I'm very happy as I am,' but the fish she had been given was particularly bony, so it came out as 'angoo, u—I'm o eawy urry agout iyig...' Even worse, she couldn't shout for help when Horace (who was quite a big dragon by now) came up behind her and grabbed her with his enormous claws, and took her up, up into the cloudless sky.

In desperation, Treasure spat the fish out and screamed, but she was too far up to be heard. She wriggled round in Horace's unyielding talons and tried to shout, 'Be careful! The weather will change any moment, it's too dangerous to fly high today!'

Clarys flapped up next to Treasure and grinned. 'Don't be silly, Treasure. It's a *beautiful* day, a light breeze and not a cloud in the sky. What do *you* know about flying anyway? Don't be scared, we've got you!'

And to prove the point, Horace let go of Treasure, but she fell only a little way before Clarys caught her with long silver claws.

Treasure tried not to show she was frightened. She gulped hard. She knew that Clarys and Horace were extremely strong and fast flyers, and Maurice never flew further than he had to, but she was sure that they were plotting something bad. But they must not play their prank today of all days! There was going to be *such* a storm that afternoon—if only she could make them believe her!

Just as she was thinking this, they flew straight into a huge bank of grey cloud, and the first heavy drops of rain landed on their noses.

Then came the thunder, and a sudden squall of wind which buffeted them from side to side, until poor, helpless Treasure began to feel sick. She had only ever been taken for little low safe flights by dear old fat Fizzle.

'I think we'd better go home!' called Clarys, passing Treasure back to Horace, but try as they might, they could not turn back. The winds were too strong, even for full-grown dragon wings and they were being blown steadily *away* from Kilve.

Hour after hour, the little dragons struggled through the wind and rain. Maurice, who was not a good flyer at the best of times, was suffering from water seeping under his untidy scales. This made him heavier and heavier. His wings were wet and began to sag. Slowly he sank until he barely skimmed the lashing waves below. He was very frightened.

Horace and Clarys were faring better, though their wings were tiring. But Treasure hung like wet seaweed from Horace's talons. When he grew tired he handed her back to Clarys. They could not keep going much longer.

Horace was all for dropping Treasure in the sea. 'No one would blame us for dropping her. If we keep going as we are, none of us will get back... If we drop her, we might just make it.'

'She didn't *ask* to be brought with us,' snapped Clarys. 'And are *you* going to be the one to explain to the Dragon Master why his beloved Treasure drowned at sea?' Horace saw the point and shut up.

At last, wet, cold and exhausted, they spotted a tall, thin, grey rock standing high above the raging seas. There was not much room for the four of them to land, but it was better than being blown hither and thither, further and further from home.

Carefully flying round the lee of the great pinnacle, they managed to find a clawhold, then very carefully they crawled up the wet, slippery, slimy rocks until they found a deep crevice where there was enough room for them all to shelter from the relentless wind.

As night fell, the cold, wet dragons managed to get to sleep, but it was a miserable night. The perpetual crashing of huge waves against the rock made their little refuge shudder. Wet spray lashed up again and again, waking them with icy water and tiny, sharp pebbles.

Wedged firmly in the little crevice, the four small dragons huddled together and cried.

The next day was no better, nor was the next night. But on the third day, the wind dropped, and the sun began to shine.

Horace, Maurice and Clarys spread out their wings to dry, and Treasure stretched out on a flat piece of rock to warm her flaking scales. They were all very hungry, but the sea still flung itself endlessly and cruelly against their rock. Now the weather had cleared, they could see the roaring, foaming tide was beating against huge broken granite teeth below. Fishing was far too dangerous. In these seas even a full-grown dragon could be dashed to pieces against those vicious rocks.

Treasure looked around at the exhausted, hopeless dragons, and felt sorry for them. Slowly and clumsily she scrambled down the rock until she found patches of seaweed flung up by the waves. There at last was the fine black purple lava weed she had been searching for. It tasted faintly fishy and, together with wild herbs that grew on the rough grass further up, it would not be a bad meal.

Carefully she gathered a large bundle of the weed, and began to carry it all the way back up to the others in her mouth. It took her the best part of the morning to gather enough for everyone. Maurice and Horace refused to eat it at first, saying it was 'muck!', but Maurice shut up when he caught the warning look in Clarys' eye. She could see Treasure had all but exhausted herself gathering the weed. Before long, even fussy Horace was eating it heartily.

Treasure was worried. She could tell by the stars that they were a long way from home. Horace had a torn wing. He could not fly far. She wrapped healing weeds around the tear, but it would take at least ten days to be strong enough for him to fly home. They would *both* have to be carried. They could not stay on the rock. They were all hungry, cold, and weak and she could tell from the smell of the wind that more storms were brewing. Things looked very dangerous.

Treasure began to think hard. She realized the others depended on her, whether they liked it or not—she could find enough food to keep them all alive for a while. She looked at the dragons. She must try not to be angry with them. They were exhausted and sleeping deeply. She wouldn't wake them, they needed their rest if they were going to survive. But she couldn't wait for them to wake either. She had a plan, and if all her instincts were right, she had to start right away...

Laboriously, Treasure collected driftwood and dried seaweed, and started to pile it at the very top of the rock. She knew she had to hurry. She could feel the tug of the next storm in the wind. By evening, the heap of wood and weed was quite big.

When the others woke, Clarys, who was feeling rather guilty, immediately helped by pulling heavy branches up to the top. Horace and Maurice simply moaned about how hungry they were, and why didn't the girls do something useful like find some food instead of building heaps of rubbish?

Treasure tried to explain what she was doing, but the boys weren't listening.

As evening fell, Treasure started to blow fire onto the heap and soon she had a great blaze glowing, lighting the sky for miles. Maurice and Horace felt cheered by the sight of flames, and they started to help by hauling more large pieces of driftwood that had been too heavy for Treasure and Clarys.

Not long before dawn, when both the fire and Treasure's hopes were getting low, they suddenly heard a shout in the skies. There above them was a flight of dragons, and on the back of Flamethrower, the strongest of them all, was the Dragon Master.

All the little dragons jumped up and down and roared great belching flames in delight. Slowly the dragons circled and came in to land, just as Treasure's bonfire died away.

The Dragon Master hugged them all, especially his little Treasure.

Clarys, who was crying hard, came and hugged Treasure too. 'Thank you, Treasure. How did you *know* to light a fire?' she asked. 'We all thought you were daft!'

Treasure shrugged and smiled. 'I knew the Dragon Master would be worried and that he would come looking for us. I just *had* to make sure he would find us.'

5
Why?

The last egg to hatch was a little shiny turquoise boy dragon called Sparky. Scarcely had the shell broken, and his long, thin snout pushed through the hole, before *trouble* began.

'Come on now, dear,' said old Pumice, who had been watching the eggs. 'Time to come out now.'

'Why?' squeaked Sparky in a cheeky little voice.

'Well...' began Pumice, who had never been asked that question before. 'Well, dear—you're ready—done—made—you know!'

Sparky pushed his long thin head out of the shell and blinked his ruby eyes at Pumice. 'Why?' he squeaked.

Pumice scratched her head with one claw and thought. 'Well, a long time ago, a Mummy dragon laid your egg to make a brand new dragon. It's taken

46

a very long time, but now you're quite ready, and much too big for your shell.' Pumice smiled. She was pleased with that answer.

'Why?' came the persistent squeak.

Pumice blinked and began to feel cross. She stretched out a long silver claw and began to pull the bits of shell off the shiny blue and green scales. 'Come *on*, dear, it's time for tea.'

'Why?'

'You must be hungry!'

Sparky thought for a second and looked interested. 'Yes, I am. Why am I?'

'Because your tummy's empty, dear, you've never had any tea before.'

'Why?'

Pumice began to shove the cheeky dragon before her, with a firm set of claws. 'Because we couldn't get fish through the shell to you.'

'Why?'

'Because it wouldn't go.'

'Why?'

By this time old Pumice had had enough. She pushed the long, thin little dragon firmly over to Flamethrower, the biggest dragon at Kilve.

'Here,' said Pumice. 'This one's called Sparky, but I'll call him *Bright* Sparky. He's impossible! You'd better find someone better-tempered than me to look after him!'

'Why?' asked Sparky, looking innocently from dragon to dragon with his gleaming little red eyes.

'He does that all the time,' said Pumice. 'Whatever you say, he interrupts with "*why*?"'

'Why?' came Sparky's silly little squeaky voice again.

'Perhaps his voice is stuck,' said Flamethrower kindly. The huge, green dragon lifted the little one onto a rock, so he could get a better look at him.

'Now, little friend, can you say my name, "Flamethrower"?'

'Why?' asked Sparky.

'Well, I want to see if your voice is stuck.'

'Why?'

'Well, if your voice *is* stuck, you'll need a doctor, but if you're just being rude, you'll need to be told off and probably sent to bed!' Flamethrower frowned at the baby.

'Why?' came the reply.

'So we can make sure you grow up into a *good* dragon,' explained Flamethrower patiently.

'Why?'

'Because that's the right thing to do.'

'Why?'

'Because that's the way the West Wind blows.'

'Why?'

Flamethrower was getting *very* cross. 'Because if you aren't good, the Rehab will come and get you!'

Sparky looked up with big wide eyes, not the least bit scared. 'Why?'

Flamethrower gritted his long, shining fangs and muttered, 'I think this one had better go to Fireworks. He's so clever, he knows the answer to everything. We've got to do *something* before . . . I lose . . . my . . . temper!'

'Why?' came the persistent little voice, as the cheeky dragon trotted obediently after Pumice and Flamethrower.

Soon they were climbing the untidy rocky path up to the clever dragon's cave. As they came into the cave mouth, there was the most terrific crash, and a puff of purple smoke belched out of the cave.

A blackened and ruffled Fireworks staggered out, grinning with all his crooked yellow teeth and looking very pleased with himself. 'I did it!' he beamed. 'I've made purple fire for the Dragon Master's birthday—he *will* be pleased!'

'Why?' came the inevitable squeak.

Fireworks stopped his jubilation and wafted the acrid smoke aside with a claw. He peered down at the baby dragon and stared.

'Who, may I ask, is this?'

'Sparky,' said Flamethrower.

'*Bright* Sparky,' added Pumice. 'He's impossible! He wants to know "*why*?" everything, and we just can't cope!'

Fireworks shook his head. 'Well, well, we must let the little ones explore and discover, otherwise they never learn, do they? All they need is a good teacher and a little patience. Never fear, we'll have him sorted out in no time!'

'Why?' squeaked Sparky as he was bustled into the untidy cave.

In the morning, an exhausted and dull-eyed Fireworks crawled out into the sunlight and blinked wearily. After him trotted the terrible Sparky, test tube in one claw and a bag of yellow powder in the other.

'But *why* can't I put this in here, Fireworks, *why*?'

'Because I've told you, it will go bang!'

'I like bangs!'

'I don't!' said Fireworks.

'Yes you do! Yes you do!' squealed Sparky, jumping up and down in glee on Fireworks' back. 'You told me so last night! You told me so!'

'Yes, but I don't like bangs *all* the time!' moaned the exhausted dragon.

'Why?'

'Because they make my head ache.'

'Why?'

'It's to do with excessive vibration in the cerebral hemispheres of the brain.'

'Why?'

'Because noise is caused by vibration, and too much vibration damages the ear drums. If the bangs are *very* loud ... or continuous,' (he added with a groan) 'it makes the cerebral hemispheres ache.' The poor dragon covered his sore head with his wings and shuddered.

' ... Why?'

'I give up!' Fireworks groaned, and finally collapsed in a sorry heap on the warm, sunny rocks.

Just to be sure of 'why?' Sparky tipped a little yellow powder into the test tube and laughed with glee at the terrific 'bang' which shook the rocks of Kilve for miles around.

All the dragons came running, hopping and flying, certain that the whole of Kilve beach, with all its caves, was about to tumble into the sea.

Flamethrower and Pumice took in the situation at once, and they scooped the bad dragon off to the cave of Fizzle, a delightful but totally deaf old dragon. He was everyone's friend, but never had the faintest idea what was going on, because he was too busy eating to bother to lip-read or learn sign language.

After a packet or two of his best chocolate biscuits, Fizzle got the idea that young Sparky needed a home for a while, just until things could be sorted out a bit.

Fizzle nodded happily and showed Sparky a nice, dry corner, with a cosy bed of freshly dried seaweed.

Every time Sparky said 'Why?' Fizzle just nodded, grinned and handed the young rascal another biscuit.

This arrangement went on happily for weeks. But because Sparky could get no questions answered in the evenings at home with Fizzle, he would ask *twice* as many during the day. The other dragons did not mind this too much, because Fizzle was very good at getting Sparky home and in bed on time, so the evenings were quite peaceful.

One day, after finding out why rocks were heavy and the wind was light, and discussing why the sky was blue and fish tasted nice, Sparky was tucking into some chocolate biscuits when the Dragon Master came to call.

'Well, young dragon, are you ready to start flying lessons soon?'

Sparky spread his fine shiny wings and looked at them. 'Why?'

'Because you're big enough to learn now.'

'Why?'

'Because you've got to learn to go fishing for yourself.'

'Why?'

'Because you're a big dragon now.'

'Why?'

'Because you eat too many chocolate biscuits.'

'Why?'

'That,' said the Dragon Master seriously, 'is a very good question.' He considered the bad little dragon carefully. 'In fact, I think you may be *too* big to learn to fly. I think it's time you came to see my wise friend, the golden dragon of the Midnight Forest.'

Ignoring the usual endless string of questions, the Dragon Master helped Sparky pack and say 'goodbye and thank you for having me' to Fizzle, and they set off.

They walked and walked, deep into the heart of the forest. Sparky was scared, but sometimes he saw something that caught his eye, and he found out about the differences between mushrooms and toadstools, foxes and foxgloves, and mountains and molehills.

At long last, they arrived at a green, moss-covered cave entrance, where, curled neatly on a warm stone in a sunny clearing, was a small, golden dragon—very different from the dragons of Kilve.

This dragon opened one emerald green eye and winked. As the Dragon Master approached, the beautiful creature uncurled his slim, smooth body, slid off his warm stone and pushed his thin head into the Dragon Master's hand.

'Greetings, Master,' he said softly. 'Whom have you brought to me?'

'This,' said the Dragon Master, 'is an impossibly inquisitive little chap called Sparky. We'd all be very grateful if he could live here with you for a little. He needs ... educating!'

Sparky was horrified. He did not want to live with a golden stranger in the middle of a darksome wood. He would miss all his friends and the sea.

'Why?' he demanded, but rather uncertainly, this time.

The strange dragon turned and peered at the mischievous little visitor. At last he stretched out his gleaming white claws and shrugged. Then with a wink and a raised eyebrow, he said simply, 'Why not?'

Sparky was so amazed he opened his mouth ...

Then he shut it again. He could not think of an answer.

6
Why Not?

Sparky looked at the small golden dragon very suspiciously for a few minutes—and the small golden dragon looked at Sparky.

'He needs to learn quite a few "why nots?" I'm afraid,' said the Dragon Master solemnly. 'I will come back soon, for he must start his flying lessons in earnest before he gets too big for his wings.'

The golden dragon considered Sparky carefully. 'Indeed, Master, you set me a very hard task indeed. But come back soon and I will have him ready for you. Farewell!' And with a flick of his gleaming tail, the golden dragon swept behind his rock and out of sight.

Horrified, Sparky turned to run to the Dragon Master, but he too was already out of sight among the trees. For the first time in his life, Sparky was alone. And what an aloneness! Lost and afraid, deep in a strange forest.

He sat down hard on the leafy ground, and felt tears stinging in his eyes. But he did not let himself cry straight away. For a few minutes, he tried to think. (This was also something he had never really done before!)

Which way had the Dragon Master gone? He had just hurried off home without even saying goodbye!

Which way had they come through the forest? Sparky had to admit to himself that he had been so intent on asking questions, he had noticed nothing about the way they had come, apart from the red toadstools which he now knew were definitely *not* for eating. But there were red toadstools *everywhere*. He could not remember the path back!

Oh, how he wished he had looked a little as well as having talked non-stop all the way!

At last, he did have a cry.

Then, when he began to run out of tears and his eyes were aching, he stopped feeling frightened and began to feel cross. 'Why? Why? Why?' he yelled into the trees, stamping hard with his large flat feet.

At this, a little voice in his ear said very softly, 'I'm afraid, my young friend, that only *you* can answer that.'

The golden dragon was curled on his rock again, and was smiling serenely through small, pointed teeth. 'Are you coming inside, or are you going to cry there all night?' he asked quietly.

Sparky looked at the sky through the trees. It was getting late. He did not fancy being outside, surrounded by woods and all sorts of strange creatures. There was nothing for it but to follow the little golden dragon.

Behind the rock where the beautiful creature had been resting was a cave entrance, almost hidden by overhanging dark green creepers and huge fronds of ferns. Sparky pushed his way inside. It was cool and dark, but rather smaller than any of the caves at Kilve.

'Get some wood from the pile at the back of the cave, please,' said the golden dragon.

'Why should I?' said Sparky sulkily.

The golden dragon just shrugged. 'You'll see why,' he smiled. Then he curled up on his favourite rocky shelf and went to sleep. Sparky found a flattish place to stretch out near the entrance, but he didn't sleep at all well.

The night was cold, and strange sounds disturbed him. Wolves came and sniffed at the cave mouth. Sparky pulled his tail inside and blew a few short blasts of flame at the intruders. But without room to beat his wings up and down, he couldn't get much fire going.

By dawn, a grey and exhausted young dragon began to see why collecting lots of firewood before going to sleep was a good idea. A roaring bonfire would have warmed him and would have kept the nosy neighbours well away.

Next morning, the golden dragon announced it was time for breakfast. Sparky looked enthusiastically around him for piles of his usual fresh-caught fish. 'Where *is* breakfast, please?' he asked as politely as possible.

'In the woods. Where should it be?' the golden dragon replied as he set off at a brisk pace.

Sparky had to trot hard to keep up. The forest was very dense and difficult for a large young dragon who was used to open spaces. Soon, they came to a clearing. The golden dragon lay still on his belly, and signalled Sparky to do the same. Suddenly with a flash of a claw, a young rabbit lay dead. Then another. Sparky looked on in dumb amazement.

The golden dragon started to eat the rabbits hungrily. Suddenly he stopped and looked at Sparky. 'Aren't you going to catch anything?' he asked.

'I... I... I've never caught a rabbit before,' he

muttered. The truth was, he'd never caught *anything* before.

'Oh, it's quite easy,' the golden dragon assured him. 'All you do is lie *quite* still, and then flash out a claw, and he's yours. Mmmm, delicious!' Then he added thoughtfully, 'But we won't take any more from *this* clearing. A few here and a few there, that's the rule.'

At last Sparky dared to venture a hesitant 'Why?'

The golden dragon smiled. 'Because if we eat all the rabbits here, it will be a long time before there are any rabbits here again.'

'I . . . I . . . don't think I fancy rabbit. I think the fur might get stuck in my teeth.'

The golden dragon smiled. 'Of course, I forgot, you're a *sea* dragon. There's a river nearby. Perhaps you fancy some fish?'

Sparky cheered up immediately, and trotted after his beautiful host. They got to the river bank. The water was swift and deep. It gleamed and glittered as it danced over the stones, leaping and foaming its way down to the sea.

Sparky looked at the golden dragon expectantly. The golden dragon looked at Sparky and smiled a little. 'Well, I'll leave you to it, shall I? I know that many dragons don't like being watched while hunting. It puts them off.' And with a wink, he slid back into the dark shadows of the forest and was gone.

Sparky looked at the water in dismay. He'd hoped the golden dragon would catch his breakfast *for* him, like the others in Kilve always did. Again, he felt the dreadful stinging of tears starting to come, and he stamped his flat foot in temper. 'WHY? It's just not fair!' he screamed. But the forest didn't answer him.

By noon, the sun was high and warming Sparky's back. He had slept a little, and now he was thirsty as well as hungry. He peered down into the water, and took a long drink. There were a few small fish, which, after a great deal of effort, he managed to lap up with his forked, scarlet tongue, but after all that effort he was hungrier than he had been before. He rested his thin head on his claws and looked longingly out towards the deep, swift centre of the river, where fat brown trout poked their round, speckled heads up, and made satisfying plopping sounds as they caught flies and slid silently down to the bottom of the water again.

'If only I could fly,' thought Sparky. 'I could skim the water gracefully and catch some of them. Horace can do it beautifully.' He stretched out his wings and looked at them. Then he folded them again. The thought of flying made him nervous.

'But I really don't understand why the golden dragon doesn't feed me. The others always did. Why did the Dragon Master leave me here like this? *Why?*'

And he started to feel very sorry for himself again. The afternoon wore on, and Sparky became hungrier and hungrier. Slowly and awkwardly, he waded into the rocky shallows at the edge of the water. He slipped and spluttered as he plunged clumsily after a few small fish that came within reach. But he splashed and stirred the water so much, he caught nothing.

As the day began to cool, Sparky began to look around, and noticed a few mushrooms, which he was certain the Dragon Master had told him *were* good to eat. They weren't very filling, but lightly toasted in dragon fire with a little wild garlic, they tasted good, and Sparky began to feel a bit better.

As the sun began to sink down low, he was getting very worried about whether the golden dragon would remember to come and get him. He had tried to watch where they were going, but it was hopeless. He was confused by all the trees. He could not remember the way back.

Just in case he was left alone, Sparky began to pile up a heap of dried wood. A night on his own in the open did not appeal, but if it had to be done, he would have the biggest bonfire ever seen in the Midnight Forest.

The golden dragon appeared just before sunset, and smiled approvingly at the bonfire waiting to be lit. 'Good, I'm glad to see you've been busy. Did you eat well?' he said. Without even waiting to hear the list of Sparky's woes, he took a large bundle of wood from the heap. 'We won't be able to carry all of this, but you did well to collect so much.' And without so much as a glance over his shoulder, the golden dragon started to glide home through the darkening shadows.

Sparky scooped up as much wood as he could carry and staggered home after his teacher.

The fire at the cave entrance burned well. No wolves came prowling, and if Sparky had not been so hungry, he would have slept very deeply.

The next day, Sparky was left by the river to catch his breakfast again. As soon as the golden tail had disappeared, Sparky waded out into the shallows, and wondered why the fish all swam away as soon as he got into the water. He thought a little, and realized that if he stayed very still, the fish might think he had gone away, then, like the golden dragon, he could flash out a claw and grab something a bit bigger than a minnow.

His plan worked well, and he was munching his second medium-sized trout when the golden dragon appeared and told him to hurry, for it was time to go.

'Why?' Sparky demanded crossly, irritated to be taken away when things were going so well at last.

The golden dragon shrugged in his usual way. 'You'll see,' he said, and walked quietly away.

Sparky had been so intent on catching fish (he was getting quite good at it, in fact) that he hadn't noticed that the sky was dark. Large, sploshy drops of rain were landing in the succulent grass on the river bank. And now he was alone again.

Sparky could see he should have followed the golden dragon straightaway and worried about 'why?' later. The rain was torrential! It clattered like a raging sea on his sodden scales. All around, the mud was thick and sticky, making walking awkward and messy.

He plodded off in the direction of where he had seen the golden dragon disappear. He was very uncertain of the way back although he *had* tried to watch and not talk. Suddenly, he noticed that the golden dragon had left claw and tail prints in the wet, muddy ground. Now he knew which way to go!

At last he reached the golden dragon's cave.

Sparky was now extremely wet and very miserable, so he curled up gratefully next to the roaring fire his host had built.

When he was rested, he began to look around, and to his delight, there was a packet of chocolate biscuits sent by Fizzle, some roast rabbit (which he found *was* delicious) and a familiar dark shape, wrapped in a magnificent deep blue cloak decorated with stars.

The Dragon Master held out a welcoming hand, and Sparky crawled over and nuzzled his best friend joyfully.

'Are you ready to come home now, by any chance?' the Dragon Master asked gently.

The little dragon looked up with sparkling eyes and grinned. With a glance at the golden dragon, he shrugged, and said, 'Why not?'

7
Nasty Dreams

It had been a wonderful summer. The evenings were long and light, with plenty of strong thermals for the dragons to bask and play in. As the warm air rose gently above the sea, the livelier dragons would catch the updraughts from the high cliff-tops to the south, then drop like stones on top of the lazy ones who were almost asleep, wings outstretched, floating on the warm breezes.

This led to furious chases southwards to the rocky pinnacles, then diving competitions to fish for crunchy lobsters deep under the almost still, clear green seas.

One evening had been such fun, and the sky was so light, that none of the young dragons wanted to go to sleep. Instead, they lit a bonfire of driftwood in a small cave overlooking the sea. There they sat, eating fish and singing songs, until it was very late.

It was then that Treasure began to tell a story. Everyone agreed that although there were many things Treasure could not do because she was wingless, she *was* a brilliant storyteller.

Treasure's story was about Leviathan, the great sea serpent who twisted herself three times around the world. Treasure said that because Leviathan was so huge and terrible, she had once eaten nearly every fish in the sea. The few that were left hid themselves so well, they could not be found.

Leviathan became *very* hungry, so she stretched her terrible, long neck out across the dry land to see what else there might be for lunch. She pushed her head above the water, and swung her huge, slimy, black-and-green-fringed jaws this way and that, left, right and all around in search of prey. Anything she met, she ate. Lions, sheep, wild boar, even a dragon or two.

The story told how at last, all the animals fled in terror to the highest point of the world. There they called as loudly as they could to the Keeper of all Beasts to seal the mouth of the monster.

And the Keeper came. Gently and firmly, he tied Leviathan's jaws with the thin wispy end of the monster's own tail. The unhappy beast could now open her great jaws only wide enough to suck in a few small shrimps at a time.

Treasure told the tale so well that when she had finished, all the dragons were huddled wide-eyed around the fire, shivering with fear.

Then Horace told a funny story about how he had chased his own tail for an hour thinking that *it* was the end of *Leviathan's* tail. The others just said that was typical, because he was stupid.

Clarys told the next story, which was about a fearsome old wizard who lived at the North Pole, and froze dragons' wings so they could never fly again. She said they stayed with the wizard as living ice statues for ever.

The little dragons were getting more and more scared, but they told Horace to shut up when he tried to tell them another funny story.

Next Clarys tried to persuade Treasure to tell the story about how Pumice lost her wings in the great fight when she defended the Dragon Master against the Behemoth. But Treasure, who was understandably a bit sensitive on the subject of wings, refused. In truth, Pumice had never told anyone what really happened.

The night was drawing in, and the chilly air wafted off the sea. The dragons pulled another pile of driftwood onto the fire. Great black shadows danced up the cave walls. Everything was silent, except for the shush of the sea on the rocks below and the light crackle of the fire burning steadily.

Very softly, Treasure began to tell another tale. It was one that the dragons had never heard before. She told a tale about a small, evil little witch who lived all alone in the depths of the Midnight Forest. 'Indeed,' said Treasure, 'it is because of her that it is called the Midnight Forest, for in the depths where she dwells, no sunlight ever comes, nor will it, until the end of time . . .'

Treasure's tale got longer and longer, and spookier and spookier, until the dragons were so scared they hardly dared to breathe.

Clarys whispered at last, 'I . . . I think I might just curl up here for the night. I think I'm too tired to walk back to my cave.' Really, she was too scared to go out into the night in case the evil little witch was hiding in a shadow, waiting for a juicy dragon supper.

Sparky, the littlest of the dragons, snuggled up to Clarys' long, sleek side, and whispered, 'I'm too scared to go out there . . .'

Maurice said in a very trembly voice that it would be fun to spend the night by the bonfire instead of going home.

Treasure frowned. 'I really ought to be getting back,' she said. 'Pumice isn't feeling well.' Then she shivered as she peered across the bay with its huge formless shadows of rock.

Suddenly, she was certain they were all slowly shifting and moving quietly up the beach towards the Forest at the behest of the witch. There was a very strange feeling in her tummy. She was beginning to wish she hadn't told the story. 'I don't think Pumice will mind if I don't go back,' she said quietly. I've slept out before ... on warm nights.'

'But this isn't warm!' said Maurice glumly. 'I'm frozen!'

'There's plenty of wood over there,' said Clarys.

'But that's over ... there!' Horace muttered, staring at the deep black gash of a shadow that ran along the cave floor between them and the wood pile. He wondered if the shadow might not really be a bottomless pit, and how deep 'bottomless' really was.

'Perhaps we should just snuggle up a bit closer,' suggested Treasure, trying to keep warm against Maurice, whose scales were always rather scratchy and lumpy, even after a thorough polishing.

Everyone was silent, listening until their ears ached for the tiny footfall of a hungry Forest Witch. The fire got lower and lower, until it was a heap of grey and red ash, but they were all too scared to cross the terrible black shadow to get to the woodpile.

At last the little dragons dozed fitfully. At about midnight, the deep black scary silence, which had been disturbed only by the noises of the sea, was suddenly shattered by the knocking of a stone against rock.

All the dragons jerked awake, and lay rigidly still and wide-eyed. They looked from one to another, terrified.

'Wassat?' whispered Clarys.

The others were too scared even to try to reply. They held their breath and shivered.

Another stone ... and a crunching footfall ...

Then again. It was *not* a dragon—it was someone far too light and *small* ... The dragons looked at each other, terrified.

They closed their bright little eyes very tightly, so they missed the look of amazement on the Dragon Master's face when he ducked under the overhanging rocks and peered into the cave.

'What *are* you all doing? The older dragons have been worried sick about you all!'

The little dragons sighed with relief at the sound of such a friendly voice. They opened their eyes and crawled (they couldn't run, the cave was too low) to meet their beloved friend. 'What *is* the matter?' he asked, stroking their beautiful scales. 'You're quite cold, all of you, and you've been sweating. Are you all ill?'

Treasure was feeling *very* guilty by this time. 'It's all my fault,' she piped, her funny little voice even squeakier than usual. 'I was telling scary stories. Then they all seemed to come real. I didn't mean to frighten anyone,' she added sadly. 'It just seemed like really good fun at the time.'

'And now we're all too scared to go back to our caves,' admitted Horace.

The Dragon Master stroked his long white beard thoughtfully and sat down. 'Put some more wood on the fire, Maurice,' he said.

Maurice looked at the black shadow doubtfully. It didn't look *quite* so deep and dark now the Dragon Master was here, but he gave a *little* jump over the 'bottomless pit', just in case.

When the fire was blazing again, and the dragons had stopped shivering, the Dragon Master held up his cloak of stars. 'Would you like me to help you sleep now? I'll tell all the other dragons you're safe.'

'Oh no!' said Clarys quickly, then, not wishing to seem ungrateful, she added: 'We'd like to, but you see, we daren't sleep. Not properly. We keep getting nasty dreams . . .'

'About the wizard from the north,' said Sparky.

'Mine's about the little witch of the Midnight Forest,' added Maurice.

'And she's coming to get me first because I made her up!' sobbed Treasure into the Dragon Master's cloak.

'I see,' said the Dragon Master kindly. 'I think you ought to tell *me* your tales, than we can see what we can do about them.'

The Dragon Master spread his cloak on the ground as he always did when a story was to be told. The little dragons gathered onto it, and the Dragon Master listened to everything. Horace even insisted on telling his tale about his tail. This made the others cross, but the Dragon Master laughed.

When they had finished, the dragons felt much better. In the bright firelight, with the Dragon Master there, the stories had lost all their strength. They were just silly little dragon tales.

The Dragon Master stroked the dragons' wings. 'If you get your fears out in the open, it often helps,' he smiled.

Treasure pushed her head under the Dragon Master's arm and looked up at him with big, wide eyes. 'But the worst of it is, I'm not just scared about the witch in my story, I know that was just pretend, but it's a different *sort* of scaryness ... I don't even know what I'm scared of, but it just sort of creeps all over me, and I can't run away from it.'

The Dragon Master stroked her scales and looked serious for a moment, then he nodded. 'What you must do, is to imagine the worst bits of your fears...'

'Must I?' shivered Treasure.

'Go on, trust me,' he said, giving her a squeeze. He tipped the little dragons from his wonderful cloak and held it up. There were no stars twinkling there now. Just empty blackness.

'Now, just make all the nasty things in your head walk into my cloak. *Make* them do it. You can!'

Then suddenly he shook his cloak into the flames of the fire. Dust and sticks and all sorts of rubbish tumbled from the black folds and caught the flames. 'Look—they've all gone!' he said.

'Now, and most important, we must put something *nice* in the space where the scaryness was, otherwise the nasties might come back.' With the merest crinkling at the corner of his kind eyes, the Dragon Master smiled as he took a jar of sweet and spicy-smelling ointment from his right-hand pocket (where he kept all his important bits and pieces) and gently rubbed a little on each dragon's nose, one at a time. As he did so, they felt safe, and warm, and they knew everything would be all right.

'And now,' he said softly, 'float on the West Wind, and you will have quiet dreams. And if nasty thoughts should creep back, just call me, for I will be here.'

Then, with a wide sweep of his arm, the Dragon Master pulled his cloak of stars over all the dragons, and they slept until the morning sun caught in their eyes.

8

'Beautifulling' Mud

Maurice had a problem. He had no sense of humour. If any one made a joke about him, he sulked for days.

This was unfortunate, because Sparky *did* have a sense of humour. And a very mischievous one at that. Sparky's favourite game was to see how many tricks he could play on Maurice, before Maurice realized he was being teased.

One day, Maurice was flying in the sunshine, doing nobody any harm. Dozily he drifted on a nice warm thermal with one eye open for a shoal of cod (dragons are *always* hungry). Just as he was almost asleep, he was very rudely poked in the ribs with a cold, scaly nose.

There was Sparky, puffing and panting, as if he'd been flying hard for hours on his fat little wings.

'Maurice,' (puff) 'Maurice, *do* slow down, I've been trying to find you all morning! I've got some really exciting news for you! Clarys and I were playing in the shallow seas north of the river, when we discovered some magic mud!'

'Magic mud?' murmured Maurice, opening one eye sceptically. 'What *sort* of magic mud? Does it grow nice, fat cod? Or maybe it sings when you can't get to sleep?'

'No, no! Nothing like that! I'm not joking—it's *beautifulling* mud!' exclaimed Sparky ecstatically. 'Clarys found it first. If you wallow in it and let it dry on you, when it cracks off, it makes your scales even more lustrous and sparkling than ever!'

Maurice's other problem was that he was vain. He wasted hours fussing over his scales, which were always dull and uneven. Every morning and night he smoothed scale polish all over them: but it did no good. He *always* looked as if he had just come back from one of Clarys' cave-crawling expeditions.

Maurice thought for a moment, his long, green head on one side.

'*Beautifulling* mud? How does it work?' he asked carefully, not wishing to look *too* interested. He didn't trust this bad little dragon, but he daren't miss the chance ... the very *slim* chance that it might be true. He flapped his wings and turned out of his thermal. He was wide awake now, and no longer thinking of dinner.

Sparky knew the only way he could keep himself from giggling and going red was to smile and look excited. 'I *told* you—it makes you beautifuller! Come and see!'

Jiggling up and down with excitement, the naughty dragon turned north-east to where a river spread out across the mudflats as it met the sea. There, the water was slimy, greasy and shallow. When the tide was out, the mud stretched as far as the eye could see. Only wading birds were happy there. It was not a place for dragons at all.

Suddenly, Sparky squeaked and nudged Maurice's tail.

'There!' he pointed with a long claw. 'Look! There, by those rocks!' Basking in the sun, at the edge of the mud, was Clarys. Her blue-green scales gleamed as if she had been oiling them for days, and her claws flashed as their silver edges caught the light. As she saw Maurice and Sparky approaching, she stretched her fine wings so Maurice could see the delicate gossamer webs shimmering.

'Oh!' exclaimed Maurice, 'You look *beautiful*!'

Clarys, who really didn't care two hoots about what she looked like, put her head on one side and grinned. 'Try the mud, Maurice. It's *bound* to do your scales some good too.'

Maurice landed on the rocks near Clarys, and regarded her first with one large, ruby eye, and then with the other. Was that a giggle at the corners of her mouth? Why wasn't she looking him straight in the eye? Was it because the sun was too bright? Could that dreadful greasy mud *really* have made her scales so shiny and colourful? There wasn't a trace of mud on her. He wasn't sure.

Slowly he walked right round her, inspecting her wings and claws. Again and again he glowered at Sparky, who was aching with the effort of not laughing.

Then he sat down on a rock near the edge of the mud and dangled the tip of his tail in the cool, smooth ooze. Tentatively, he drew it up and considered the effect. It was now a nasty greeny-brown colour. And it stank!

Suddenly, his claws slipped on the greasy mud puddle left by his tail. With a pitiful howl he slithered right down the rocks into the dark, smelly mud. Slop! Slurp! Splat!

Terrified, Maurice floundered so wildly that stinking, oozing splashes of mud smothered Clarys and Sparky from head to claw. They screamed with disgust.

Then out from the mud's edge appeared a greeny-blackish shape, slowly, nastily slithering and scraping out of the slime. Maurice blinked out from under the stinking mass, and his angry red eyes glowed menacingly at Clarys and Sparky.

The two little dragons were not laughing now. Slowly they backed away from this terrible slimy monster that was coming to get them. But they weren't fast enough. Suddenly, with a great bellow, the angry Maurice shook himself hard like a dog, and foul mud splattered and sprayed everywhere!

Mud trickled down snouts, into eyes, over tongues and along backs. All three of them were cold, wet and miserable. But worst of all, the mud was all over their wings! Of course, dragons can fly only if their wings are kept absolutely clean. If the webs are torn or wet, flight is difficult, but if they get muddy—it is impossible.

At first the three little dragons stared at each other in silent rage.

'Now look at what you've done!' muttered Maurice, snorting enormous dark green, noisy bubbles through his nose as he tried to talk.

'*We* can't help it if you're a clumsy oaf!' roared Clarys, 'How did we know you'd dance around the edge of the mud as if it was the middle of a field? It's not *our* fault you fell in!'

'Yes, but you were trying to *get* me in, weren't you?' glowered Maurice, lowering his slimy mud-green head and making his red eyes bulge out at her.

'Not really—no!' she snapped, keeping her claws crossed, because she was lying.

'I've got a good mind to go and push you two right in, and hold you under for a whole week!' roared Maurice, looking at his nasty, smelly wings, and trying hard not to cry.

Sparky suddenly realized it was getting dark and said quietly, 'I think we had better be getting back, don't you? If we keep on like this, we're going to be stuck out here all night.'

The other two stopped arguing. He was right. 'Let's try and find some clean water. If we can get this muck off, there's a chance we can fly home before dark.'

Sulkily and silently, the three dragons trudged southward, hoping to find cleaner seas as they got nearer home. It grew darker and darker. The wind became colder and colder. Even worse, the tide was coming in, and the ground was becoming marshier and soggier. At last they found they were on a little island of muddy tussocks and reeds. There was no hope of getting any further that night.

It was cold and lonely for the three little dragons on those marshes. Worst of all, it is very difficult to cuddle up to someone if you are angry with them. And Maurice, Clarys and Sparky were all *very* angry.

Clarys was cross with Sparky for having thought up the daft idea in the first place, and with Maurice for having sprayed her with mud.

Sparky was angry with Maurice too, but he also wished Clarys had not insisted on going to the mud flats to play the joke. It was a very long way from home.

Understandably, Maurice was angry about the whole situation. Mostly, he was cross with himself for having been stupid enough to have gone to look for 'beautifulling' mud in the first place.

It was a long, cold, miserable night.

When the wind was at its coldest, a few 'I'm sorries' were whispered, and they all curled up together and felt a little warmer. But only a little. The sound of water hissing through the reeds made them shiver, and soon their tails were dangling in icy wetness.

'Do you know what?' said Clarys miserably.

'What?' muttered an unhappy Maurice.

'I can't decide if the Dragon Master is the first or last person I want to see right now.'

'I know what you mean,' moaned Sparky. 'I want to see him because then I know everything will be all right. But I know that when I *do* see him, I'll feel awful. I'll want to run and hide, because of what we've been up to.'

There was silence, then from a little way off came a soft voice: 'Please make up your minds, young dragons. Do you want to see me or not? I'm freezing too.'

'Dragon Master!' they all called at once, scrambling and slipping in the icy mud. 'Help! Where are you?'

'I'm here.' And the Dragon Master lit a little glow of fire, so the little dragons could see their cold, wet much-loved friend standing on a rock not far away.

'I've been thinking,' he said. 'You are so big and heavy, it's too dangerous for you to cross to the bank here while it's still dark. But you're safe for the moment. The tide is going down now. I think I had better try and get across to you ... if you want me to?'

'Oh, we want you. Please do try, Dragon Master, we're so cold and unhappy!' sobbed Clarys.

The Dragon Master scooped up the long edge of his deep blue robe, and tied his wonderful cloak into a bundle. Then with the help of his light, he stepped tentatively from muddy tussock to reedy patch, until he reached the dragons.

Then all three of them started talking at once: 'We've had an *awful* time,' they said. 'Sparky was telling Maurice ... and Clarys was pretending ... and Maurice fell in the mud ...'

'It's all my fault,' said Sparky, 'I just can't help teasing Maurice.'

'But it was me who thought up the plan,' moaned Clarys.

'And if I hadn't been so worried about my looks, I'd never have fallen for their stupid trick,' groaned Maurice.

'And we're all very sorry and we're *so* glad to see you!' The shivering little dragons huddled under the Dragon Master's enormous cloak, and felt much, much better.

The Dragon Master, who was trying to listen to them all at once, pulled them closer together and organized their tails so they didn't trail in the cold water.

'I've been looking for you three scallywags since sunset,' he said quietly, stroking their wings. 'And I'll stay with you now I've found you. I've told Ember and Flamethrower to come searching for us at first light. They'll be here soon, I should think.'

When dawn came, the sight of the dragonflight above made everyone cheer. The great dragons soon had everyone home.

It took hours of swimming in the sea, and being rubbed down with Pumice's special soapweeds, to get the little dragons clean again. Even the Dragon Master had to have a bath, but he insisted that Fireworks heated up a rock pool in a cave for him. He said he had had enough of cold water for a very long time.

When all four of them were clean and warming themselves by a roaring driftwood fire in Pumice's cave, the Dragon Master peered under his bushy eyebrows at Maurice, Clarys and Sparky. The three little dragons felt *very* uncomfortable.

'Here goes,' thought Maurice. 'Now for the trouble.'

But the Dragon Master was smiling. 'I don't think you three *need* to be told off, do you?' he said softly.

The miserable dragons stared in disbelief. This wasn't what they'd expected at all. They shook their heads, mouths open wide in amazement.

'Then go out and play and don't be so silly again, *any* of you! Go on! Shoo!' the Dragon Master laughed, clapping his hands.

With just the *merest* glance in a rock pool to see if his scales were tidy, Maurice led the others out of the cave and into the fresh, welcoming sunshine.

Then Maurice, Clarys and Sparky stretched out their clean, sparkling wings and lifted themselves gracefully up into the sky.

9
Flying the West Wind

One cool evening in the autumn, Pumice, the old, wingless dragon, dragged herself into her cave and lay still. She did not feel very well at all. She had been busy all day, trying to tidy her cave.

The other dragons could fly here, there and everywhere. But poor old Pumice had to walk. She had lost her wings centuries before, when she had fought the Behemoth.

Now she was tired.

There was a scraping noise at the entrance. It was Treasure, the little wingless dragon, coming home with a heavy load of seaweed. Treasure and Pumice lived together, helping each other as they could.

That night, the cave felt chilly and dark. Treasure lit a fire and coaxed Pumice to eat some fish. As dark fell, Treasure began to feel alone and frightened, though Pumice was stretched out beside her. She piled fresh dried seaweed over her old friend, and curled up next to her to sleep.

In the morning, Pumice didn't speak or move. Her dragonfire was out.

Distraught, Treasure ran out into the cold wind and rain. She needed the Dragon Master! Where was he? High over rocks, and wide over the hills she ran, calling and searching, frantic and frightened.

Suddenly, she stopped and thought.

'Why am I running so far and so fast? He has always been around when we really needed him. He even managed to find us when we were stranded on the rock in the sea. I'm doing this all wrong. I will go back home and just wait.'

Wearily, she dragged her way back to the cave.

It was cold and dark inside.

And still.

Treasure sat down next to Pumice and cried. She was feeling so lost and alone. The other dragons had gone for their morning flight to catch fish. It wouldn't be long before Igneous and Furnace brought something for her ... and Pumice. Oh, how she wished they would hurry!

The Dragon Master came quietly into the cave. He put his warm hand on Treasure's head and stroked her gently. Slowly, she stopped crying.

'I'm glad you came back,' he said. 'I wasn't far away.' Then, together, they knelt next to the still, grey shape of Pumice stretched out along the floor. Despite Treasure's best efforts, Pumice was quite cold.

'Her dragonfire has gone out,' Treasure said softly, stroking her friend's head. 'Light it again for her, Dragon Master. Please. She needs her warmth. She's so old and tired.'

The Dragon Master wiped a tear away, and in a choking sort of a voice, he whispered. 'Indeed, little one, her dragonfire *has* gone out. It will never light again. She is dead.'

Treasure sat still and silent. Then, 'Call the West Wind to blow her back to us again!' she begged urgently. '*Please!*'

The Dragon Master smiled a little and stroked Treasure's smooth green and blue scales. 'Indeed, these things *are* possible. But what would happen if I *did* call her back from flying the West Wind? She would be cold again, and ache in every joint. The pain of where her wings were burned would come back.'

'But she's so cold! She must ache even more now her dragonfire has gone!'

The Dragon Master kissed Treasure on the nose. 'No, all of that is over. She is with the West Wind that blows beyond everything. She is flying as only those who are within the Wind know how. You will see what I mean later, but for now, here come the other dragons to weep with you and for you. Have a good cry. Pour it all out,' said the Dragon Master kindly.

Then leaning against the cold, smooth sides of the great dragoness, he wept too.

Pumice's funeral was sad and beautiful.

Each dragon came, one at a time, and stood next to Pumice. Then he or she sang a song of the winds and the air, or told a tale of the sea and the ceaseless waves. Each dragon had something to say about Pumice: something good that she had done or a little memory of how special she had been.

Pumice had been taken to lie on the seashore. Lovingly she had been surrounded by posies of autumn flowers woven with ribbons of seaweed. Shells were threaded and arranged in twisting patterns all around her long, grey-blue sides.

Treasure could not help thinking that Pumice must be cold and lonely. So she wept. She felt cold and lonely too.

At last, all the dragons had said something. There was silence.

'It's your turn,' said Flamethrower softly, gently

nudging Treasure forward with his long nose. She felt so scared and small. She couldn't say anything.

Suddenly she hugged Pumice. Dear old Pumice who had loved her little Treasure and looked after her, when everyone else had said a wingless dragon would be useless.

'Thank you,' she whispered in the old dragon's ear. 'I love you. I know I never said that before, but I hope you can still hear in the West Wind.' She kissed the old, kind, tired face. 'I don't want you to hurt or to ache any more, I want you to fly again... Goodbye. Fly well.'

And with that, the Dragon Master said very softly, 'Let us all give her to the Wind. She was born of fire and wind, and by fire and wind she will return.'

All the dragons breathed softly, and the glowing, blood-red flames caressed and warmed the old dragon's bones.

When all was over, Flamethrower took Treasure back to his cave, and gave her the best bed of dried seaweed. He offered her supper of roast shark, but she couldn't eat. Silently, she lay down and closed her dark red eyes which burned and stung with tears.

Something woke her suddenly.

The night was quite dark. It was the Dragon

Master. He was stroking her ears. In a soft voice he whispered, 'Treasure, Treasure, come with me. We will leave the other dragons for a little, and rest. We are both aching.' They walked a little way until they felt the cool, fresh West Wind on their backs. Then together, they both rose into the night sky, and flew.

On, on, towards the rising sun, they went, over land and sea. Deep blue sky gave way to lighter hues. Streaks of pink and gold coloured the clouds.

Steadily, they flew, all the time being chased and carried by the West Wind.

High over a great ocean, the wind gained strength, buffeting and tossing the travellers like bits of down on a stormy sea. But Treasure, who usually hated flying, felt no fear. The Wind spun them round and round, then came from behind, below, above. They were blown high, then caught, tossed and captured. The little dragon and her friend rolled and span, felt safe, but were scared, all at once.

Slowly, the Wind swept them on and on. Higher, and higher they went, until the sky became dark again: then black with piercing icy lights of stars and suns and constellations without number. At last, another light began to grow. It was like dawn, but softer and gentler.

It was a strange sort of a light. Treasure felt as if it were alive and warm.

She lay still, floating and quiet. Softly and slowly they were cradled by the West Wind that blows beyond everything.

Quiet. Safe. No pain. No grief.

Suddenly Treasure leapt up, laughing and leaping as if she was a hatchling gone dizzy with her first flight. Everything was so full and alive ... *She* was alive! She could do *anything*. She would go with the Wind wherever it blew! She was *in* the Wind, and it was *in* her.

She did not know where or how, and cared even less.

Suddenly, her dancing stopped.

There ... was Pumice.

She was no longer grey, but shimmering greeny-blue and alive, with great strong silver wings that stretched triumphantly high above her.

Silently, Pumice touched her little Treasure with her warm nose, and smiled. It was the touch of real dragonfire, the fire from which they had all been born, and all around them was the tossing laughter of the West Wind.

Treasure did not remember flying back to her cave. She only remembered feeling the Dragon

Master kiss her on the nose as he told her to sleep again.

In the morning, she woke and ate cold roast shark before going for a morning swim.

The Dragon Master met her on the shore and they walked to dry Treasure's scales.

'I'm glad you took me with you last night,' she said. 'I've still got a lot of crying to do ... Pumice being dead still hurts a lot. But at least I'm not frightened any more.'

'I feel better too,' said the Dragon Master. Then the two friends sat and squeezed hand and claw, and were silent for a very long time.

10
How Pumice Lost Her Wings

After Pumice died, everyone felt very sad.

One day, the Dragon Master came and spread out his wonderful cloak so the little dragons could come and sit next to him. The bigger dragons lay close by, sunning themselves on the rocks.

The Dragon Master's cloak was very special. If he spread it out at night, the stars came out, and wonderful dreams filled the dragons' heads. When he spread the cloak during the day, it meant they were about to hear the most wonderful tales.

The Dragon Master smiled at his friends as he stroked their blue-green scales in the sunshine. 'Today you will hear a very special story,' he said. 'Since the day this terrible thing took place, Pumice the great dragoness forbade the telling of the tale. But now is the time to honour her as she deserves. I have entrusted the words to Treasure. I would like her to do the telling, as she has taken Pumice's place among us.'

Treasure sat, tail curled and head held high, right in the middle of the Dragon Master's cloak. Her voice was a bit squeaky at first, but soon, no one noticed. For this was the story of how Pumice lost her wings.

'Long, long years ago, when the Creator made wind and fire burn together to make the world, many strange creatures came forth. Each one was given a special friend, a Master or a Mistress to help them in their great task, and to guard them from evil.

'The terrible serpent Leviathan has her Mistress, as do the wild unicorns. The Behemoth has his Master.

'The task of the Behemoth was to guard the secrets of the boiling depths of the world. There, in the ever-seething ocean of molten lava, he was king.

'One day, the monster looked out of a volcano crater, and saw the soft green world above. Everything there was peaceful and pleasant. The Behemoth became very angry and jealous. Here was a whole world which did not call him king. He would burn it and make it hot and empty. Then it would all be his.

'The Behemoth Master wanted power for himself too. He wanted to use the secrets of the earth to rule over the unicorns, Leviathan and even the dragons...

'So between them, they decided to make a war.

'In those days, Flamethrower was only a hatchling and Fizzle could hear a worm wriggle on the next continent, his hearing was so sharp.'

'That *must* have been a long time ago!' muttered Sparky.

Ember, who was herself hardly hatched in those days, poked the young dragon with a firm claw and hissed at him to be quiet.

Treasure continued. 'In those days Pumice was a cross little girl dragon, with little else to do except eat fish and moan. Nothing was ever good enough for her, and nothing was ever right. She had beautiful silver wings and she loved it when everyone admired them.

'It was nothing to her that the war raged on, with the terrible burning of forests by the great Behemoth, and the evil magic woven by his treacherous Master from the deep secrets entrusted to him by the Creator.

'One day, word came that the battle was raging towards our land. It was said that as the monster and his Master came, they belched fire, ripped up rocks and crashed continents into one another. Wherever they went, the face of the earth was scorched and changed beyond all recognition.

'All the dragons, even the little ones, flew to try to turn the Behemoth back before he reached the Midnight Forest. They had to protect all the animals and trees!

'Only one dragon didn't go to the battle. That was fussy little Pumice, who sat in the back of her cave and sulked. She felt the others ought to be at home, looking after *her*. She didn't see there was any point whatsoever in chasing after things like Behemoths. She thought *that* was the Dragon Master's job.

'For long days and nights, she sat in her cave by the sea, wishing the noise of battle would go away, and that someone would come and look after her.

'At long last, someone *did* come, but not anyone Pumice had ever seen before. Some of the slimy silver-grey wood creatures that live under fallen tree trunks and down little holes in the Midnight Forest came to her cave.

'Pumice was curled up at the back of the cave when the creatures arrived, so they did not see her. She wasn't sure whether they were friendly or not, so she stayed quite still and listened to what they were saying.

' "I don't understand where the dragons of Kilve can be," said one.

' "The Master will kill us if we don't find them," said another.

' "No, he won't," said a third, "He'll pull our wings and legs off, one by one, just as he promised."

'The others fell silent and shivered at the thought of such a terrible fate.

'Pumice shrank back, well out of sight. She felt cold and afraid. She was certain they weren't talking about the *Dragon* Master. He would never do anything like that.

' "Well, where *are* the dragons?" repeated the first creature. ' "We have to find them quickly. It is only them and their silly Dragon Master who stand in the way of our Master's total victory. If we succeed, tomorrow we will be rewarded handsomely indeed."

' "Tomorrow we'll be wingless and legless if we don't find the dragons. We must distract them from what our Master intends to do. Our orders are to keep the dragons busy here, so the Behemoth can burn the Midnight Forest and his Master can tackle that dreadful Dragon Master. Soon the whole world will be a burning desert and the Behemoth will be king."

' "I don't remember the Dragon Master being that

dreadful," piped up the third creature. "I remember him being ... kind ... understanding."

' "Bah! He's nothing compared to *our* Master!" scoffed the second creature. "The Behemoth and his Master know ..." and here he leaned over and whispered ... "*secrets* ... I've seen ... and heard!"

' "What sort of secrets?" gasped the others.

' "Secrets from the depths of the earth. Secrets from before time began—*special* secrets that the wishy-washy Dragon Master knows nothing of ..."

' "Tell us! Tell us!" begged the others.

' "No!" he snapped. "These things are forbidden to all but the powerful! Now. Let us eat and rest here. The dragons must be out hunting. They will return soon and we must be ready for them."

'Pumice sat rigidly still for a few minutes, then she made up her mind. She must find the Dragon Master and warn him. Even *she* could see that events affected her at last. And she was the only one who could help.

'Pumice knew that at the back of the cave there was was a tiny crack which led along an underground passage some way inland. She had often explored it when she was very tiny. It was tight then. She knew she had little chance of getting through it now she was older and bigger. But she had to try. Short of fighting the woodland creatures (and their teeth looked *very* sharp) it was the only way.

'Luckily, Pumice had sat in the cave sulking for so long, and had eaten so little, that she had become very thin. With only a few scrapes and cuts, she soon found herself standing on a windy inland hillside, well out of sight of Kilve.

'But how could she find the Dragon Master? She had been on her own for days. She didn't even know where Flamethrower or Fizzle were. She had never felt so alone.

'She tried to roar and breathe fire to make herself feel brave, but tears trickled down her nose and put her flames out, leaving nasty-tasting smoke in her mouth. So, with a deep breath, Pumice stretched her beautiful silver wings in the sunlight, and flew up and up, circling higher and higher into the sky.

'Far below the sea sparkled grey and green, then as she wheeled inland, she saw smoke rising over the farthest reaches of the Midnight Forest. She set her course that way, then she began to think.

'If there was trouble ahead, it would be wise not to be seen. Everything depended on her getting to the others secretly, so she could tell what she knew. A little higher, grey clouds were mounting and dancing inland on a stiff westerly breeze. She had never flown that high before, but up she went, hovering near the base of the clouds. From there she could see down below, but she would not be easily spotted from the ground.

'Soon she could see the cause of the smoke. The dragons were there, locked in a terrible fire-battle with all sorts of creatures that she had never seen before—animals of the deepest earth—they must be friends of the Behemoth! As the clouds she was hiding in flew past the battle, she had to decide whether to break cover and try to reach her friends.

'But something told her to keep going. On and on she flew. The clouds around her became thicker and blacker, until she could hardly see. A stench of burning and sulphur began to fill the air, and Pumice began to choke. But she kept going, until at last, she heard a shout. It was a voice she knew! Could it be the Dragon Master?

'"Coming!" she tried to call, but the words stuck in her throat as the choking smoke began to fill her lungs. Down she plummeted, until she began to feel that there were walls around her. The air became thicker with fumes. Everything was completely black.

'Was that another shout? She speeded her steep spiral down until she saw a glow of fire, and felt heat on her belly and wings. She was flying into the heart of a volcano!

'As she plummeted, the glowing heat became worse, but she called again. There—a reply! It *was* the Dragon Master! He was trapped below in the crater.

'Soon, in the terrible glare of the boiling lava below, she saw him, standing on a ledge, faced by the huge, heaving bulk of the Behemoth. The monster was too terrible to describe. His feet were in the molten lava, and his huge head was level with his captive. His eyes and teeth glinted with glee.

'On the monster's shoulder stood his evil Master, swathed in a blood-red cloak. The Master's face and eyes were mean and cruel. He had his arms raised. In one hand he carried a short staff. He seemed to be chanting. Venom and resentment spat in his voice. Pumice guessed he was using one of his strange secrets against her friend.

The Dragon Master had his dark blue cloak of stars wrapped tightly around him. His wild hair was thrown back and shining blood red from the glowing fires. He was trapped and afraid, but his voice sounded clear and strong above the terrible roar of the volcano and the insistent howling of the beast.

' "I don't want your secrets!" he said. "They are poisonous!"

'The Behemoth Master threw back his head and laughed horribly. "But if you don't take my secrets, then I will kill you now. All your precious little dragons will be in my power by tonight!

'Through the smoke and gloom, Pumice saw the Dragon Master look up, as if searching for a chink of real light amid the searing fireglow. "Come, West Wind, and blow," he called clearly.

Pumice didn't hesitate. Swiftly she adjusted her flightpath and swooped from behind. Then, with one flick of her wing, she knocked the Behemoth Master into the boiling lava, way below. He fell for a long time, until he was only a black, spinning dot against the boiling red and white heat. Then he had gone.

'The Behemoth stared stupidly below. He didn't seem to understand what was happening at all. Without his Master, he was only a great lumbering beast.

'Swiftly, Pumice landed next to the Dragon Master, who clambered wearily onto her back. She barely waited long enough for him to mount before she began her great ascent. Up, up, she flew, climbing towards the sky that she knew was somewhere up above. She could hardly breathe and her wings and belly were burning with agonizing heat.

'Terrified, she suddenly realized that the Dragon Master was too heavy for her. She could fly no more. She was exhausted and suffocating . . .

' "Help!" she called weakly and hopelessly into the stinking dark.

'Suddenly from below came a mightly roar, as the Behemoth realized that he had been robbed of both his Master and his prey by a small, thin dragon.

'With a howl, he let out a terrible belch of flames and smoke, which caught Pumice in its full force.

'But the blast also blew them upwards and out into the open air! With what fragments were left of her wings, Pumice managed to glide to a safe landing on cool, green grass.'

Treasure stopped and swallowed hard. It was difficult for her not to cry, so the Dragon Master took up the tale.

'It was there,' he said, 'that we were found by the Mistress of the Unicorns. Her wonderful creatures have the power to heal with one touch of their horns. With the help of this lady and her beasts, I recovered quickly, but what was left of Pumice's wings had to be cut off, and the unicorns healed the stumps. Then they ran to find the other dragons, so we could be carried back to Kilve.'

There was a long silence.

At last Maurice whistled. 'Fancy Pumice killing the Behemoth Master! We never realized she was so special.'

The Dragon Master smiled and rubbed Maurice's scales in that nice scratchy place between the wings. 'She was no different from you. Pumice was just a sulky little dragon who wouldn't clean her cave. When the time came, she saw something she had to do and she did it . . .'

And with that, the Dragon Master stood up and shook out his long dark blue cloak, spilling little dragons everywhere. 'And talking of time, the sun is setting. It is time I lit the stars, and sent you lot home to bed!'

And he did.

11
The Day
the Rehab Came

Winter passed and the days grew long again. The fishing was good, and the skies were warm. The dragons grew fat and contented. No one argued, no one played nasty, muddy tricks on anyone else, and Sparky hadn't asked 'why?' for a whole week.

'I wish it was like this all the time,' said Horace.

'Someone's bound to spoil it!' said Maurice.

'It's bound to be Clarys,' said Horace.

'Why?' asked Sparky innocently.

Clarys was wondering whose tail to twist first, Horace's for being rude, or Sparky's for saying 'Why?' when the Dragon Master came puffing and panting up the slope.

He sat down on the grass near the cliff edge, overlooking the sea. Then he spread his wonderful cloak around him so the little dragons could come and sit next to him. He usually did this when he was about to tell a story, so the dragons were pleased.

But there was no story. He looked very serious.

'I fear the Rehab is coming,' he said sadly.

The dragons looked at each other. They were very worried. They'd only heard of the Rehab once or twice before and they had no idea what it was, but they knew it meant trouble.

The Dragon Master went on. 'The Rehab is a terrible sea monster. He is not very big. In fact, it is sometimes difficult to spot him. But when he comes, it is very bad news.'

'What does he *do*?' asked the little dragons.

'He turns everything inside out and upside down,' said the Dragon Master sadly. 'He brings chaos.'

'Like my cave?' chirped Sparky.

The others promptly sat on him to make him shut up, but the Dragon Master smiled. 'Let him go. We're going to need every dragon we've got— even naughty little ones,' he said.

The day the Rehab came was still. Not just calm, but deadly still. For days, the birds had been wheeling and crying overhead, fleeing inland. Now they had all gone. The skies were silent. Most of the fish had swum away. The animals that lived in the hills had slipped deeper into the Midnight Forest.

And worst of all, the Dragon Master hadn't been seen for days.

The dragons felt very worried.

At last, it happened. At first it looked as if the sea were throwing up a huge tidal wave from the north. A distant soft rumble grew and filled the air with a horrible howling and rushing of waves and wind, and a crunching and crashing of splintering rocks.

Closer and closer it came, until the sky seemed to be filled with the sea, and the sea bed was full of broken plants and trees. Indeed, everything *was* upside down and inside out.

Terrified, the dragons gathered together in a huddle on top of the highest cliff, and waited.

Suddenly Clarys snapped at Sparky for treading on her tail. Horace stepped out of Clarys' way and pushed Maurice downhill by accident. Maurice scrambled back up and started to scratch at Horace, and Flamethrower and Fireworks started to argue about who should stand where.

The old deaf dragon, Fizzle, kept eating his chocolate biscuits, ignoring everything that was going on, until Sparky told him very slowly and clearly that he was a deaf old fool. Sparky was cuffed firmly around the ear, and Treasure told Sparky he was a stupid little baby. Igneous and Furnace threatened to set the place alight if everyone didn't stop arguing.

'Stop it! *STOP IT!*' roared Flamethrower, spitting orange fire. 'What *would* the Dragon Master say?'

Everyone stopped shouting and felt uncomfortable. They shuffled from foot to foot and looked embarrassed. Clarys said it was Horace's fault. Furnace said it was Sparky who has started it. Igneous said it was Maurice, and he'd never liked any of them anyway, and Treasure began to cry.

While they were arguing, the strange storm stopped. In the silence between the argument and the wind, a little sneering, giggly voice said, 'Hello. I'm Rehab. I've come to see you.'

There, in the grass, was a small, grey slug. And it was laughing!

Furious, all the dragons tried to stamp on it. But they all rushed to the same spot so hard and fast and suddenly, that all their heads collided with a terrible *crash*. Stunned and aching, they staggered back and glared angrily at each other.

Suddenly, Maurice noticed that the small slugthing wasn't there. It had crawled up a nearby tree, where it could laugh at the dragons with a better view. And it was a little bigger than it had been.

Again, the dragons rushed at it, only to collide with the tree, tangle their wings and bump their heads again.

'Stand back!' ordered Igneous, belching a huge ball of fire at the tree. This only succeeded in reducing the tree and several shrubs to ashes, and scorching Flamethrower's wings in the process.

The big old dragon was furious. He dived with bared teeth and claws at Igneous. If it hadn't been for Treasure standing in his way, he'd have done terrible things to the young dragon.

'STOP!' yelled Treasure at the top of her voice. 'Can't you *see* what's happening? *We've* been turned inside out too. Rehab has got *between* us!'

Nonsense!' said Igneous. 'I've just reduced him to ashes!'

'No, she's right,' said Flamethrower. 'Look!'

And there, on the grass, were thick, slimy slug tracks, weaving in and out, up and down, all around them. There were even glistening trails all over their beautiful scales.

'Ugh!' said Maurice, who spent all his time polishing his scales. And he began to wipe at the slime with bundles of grass. But it did no good, it only spread the slime further, and made Maurice crosser than ever.

And there, right in front of them, sat a fat, grey slug, now almost the size of a cat. And it was *still* laughing in its horrid mocking way.

The dragons were about to lurch at him again,

when Treasure piped up: 'Look, can't you *see*? He gets fatter on us arguing. The more we try to all rush to kill him at once, the more we hurt each other, and *that* makes everything worse! It's not each other we have to fight, it's *him!*'

'She's right,' said Flamethrower. 'Igneous, you and I have the strongest dragonfire. Together we will burn this thing to cinders!'

The other dragons drew back, knowing that between them the great dragons could destroy everything for miles.

There was silence, except for a silly, high, giggling noise from the creature.

Then came the moment! Flamethrower and Igneous blew their dragonfire as hard as they could! But the Rehab had disappeared, and instead of orange and red flames, only *water* poured out of the huge, red, dragon nostrils. All the other dragons laughed cruelly. The great dragons flashed their claws at the others and lashed their tails furiously.

Treasure begged everyone to be silent.

'We must concentrate on the Rehab,' warned Flamethrower.

Then Horace spoke up. 'I can fly very high and very fast. Shall I take this Rehab thing in my talons and drop it somewhere a very long way away?'

Everyone agreed that would be an excellent idea.

Horace advanced tentatively on the grey shape. The Rehab was getting bigger and laughing more loudly every minute. With a quick snatch, Horace had the thing in his claws and had launched himself high into the clouds. But the harder Horace flew, the more he found he was getting nowhere. He struggled and struggled, flapped and wheeled, but he had hardly left the space above the hillside. Suddenly, he was sucked down, down, until he fell in an exhausted heap, upside down on his back, and covered in thick, grey slime. Gleefully, the Rehab wriggled out from the dragon's claws, laughing more loudly than ever.

And there was still no sign of the Dragon Master.

The dragons were very frightened and worried. They couldn't think what to do.

Treasure called them all into a huddle, well away from the creature, which was getting bigger and bigger every second. It would soon be as big as Sparky.

'We've tried all *our* weapons,' she said, 'but we haven't thought about what *his* weapons are.'

'Slime!' said Maurice.

'And horrid, malicious laughter,' said Clarys.

'What can we do against *that*?' asked Flame-thrower.

'We can put wax in our ears,' said Furnace.

'That's a good idea,' said Treasure, 'but we'll have to finish our council of war first.'

'I wish the Dragon Master were here,' moaned Clarys.

'Well, he's not!' said Flamethrower. 'We've just got to do our best and not let it matter.'

'You're right!' said Treasure. 'Now, the other thing that Rehab does is to turn things inside out. When he's around, we argue. He makes tiny accidents feel like terrible crimes.'

'And he turned the sky into the sea and the sea into the sky,' added Maurice.

'And he stopped me from flying,' said Horace, frightened. 'He turned my flying into a horrid sucking-dropping sort of thing.'

'So,' said Treasure, 'if he turns everything inside out, how can we use our own weapons *against* him?'

'Stamp on him?' suggested Fireworks.

'No!' everyone shouted.

'Perhaps I could ask him why he's doing it?' suggested Sparky doubtfully.

Treasure looked at him with interest. 'Go on,' she said. 'Try it. It might give us a clue.'

Sparky looked worried. Suddenly his stomach was in a burning knot. He was scared. 'Dare I?' he asked.

'You're the only only who can,' Treasure replied.

Slowly, Sparky walked over to the Rehab-slug-thing and looked down at it. It looked a bit smaller now. That was comforting, although it was still giggling, but in a rather worried way, with its mouth wide open. Sparky noticed it hadn't cleaned its teeth. What a grimy little monster!

Sparky took a step forward. The Rehab took a step back. Sparky took another step forward. The Rehab took another step back. Sparky looked down at the slug, first out of one eye, then out of the other.

'Excuse me ... sir,' he said doubtfully. 'Why are you doing this?'

The slug looked up and just sneered. 'Because you all think you're so big and important with your posh scales and fancy wings. But you're nothing. Nothing!' And he spat at Sparky.

'But that's not true!' said Sparky, beginning to cry. 'It's just not true!'

As he spoke, the slug became smaller and smaller. One by one, the other dragons came and stood next to Sparky, looking down at the small, grey slug in the grass.

'You're stupid. You're nothing, the lot of you!' it squeaked.

'We may often be stupid,' said Flamethrower

carefully, 'but the Dragon Master loves us just as we are, so we can't be nothing.'

And with that, the Rehab shrivelled and shrank like a soft balloon with a hole in it. With a quick wiggle, he slid back into the sea, and with the smallest of splashes he was gone.

It was then the Dragon Master appeared, climbing slowly up the hill.

'Oh, Dragon Master!' they all shouted, tumbling down the slope towards their friend. 'We do wish you'd been here, we've had such a *terrible* time!'

'Of course I was here,' said the Dragon Master gently. 'But if you'd been able to see me, you'd have expected me to fight *for* you, like baby dragons. You had to learn to fight the Rehab for yourselves.

'You found that squashing, dropping and blasting him just didn't work. Whatever you did turned upside down out and inside out. That made you furious—and that made the Rehab bigger and stronger. You couldn't win.

'But when we stopped arguing and found out *why* he was sneering at us, we knew it wasn't true . . .' said Sparky.

'And that made him shrivel up!' roared Horace in delight, sending warm red flames up into the sky.

12
Treasure Hunt

The Dragon Master had a secret. No one knew what it was, but they guessed something very important was about to happen, for he had told everyone to get ready for a very big party.

For days on end, the dragons had been collecting wood and seaweed to make a huge bonfire on a flat, wide space just above the high tide mark.

Fireworks was mixing special powders to make a magnificent coloured smoke display. Maurice and Sparky were planning an aerobatic fly-past and, as a special treat, Flamethrower and Ember were to sing!

It was all very exciting. Everyone was so busy catching small basking sharks to eat and making herb sauces and seaweed breads, no one stopped to wonder why such a magnificent party was being held at all. It wasn't even the Dragon Master's birthday.

At last, the evening of the party came. Everyone drank and ate and flew and danced and sang, until dawn began to show above the inland hills. The dragons sat quiet and still near the dying embers of the fire.

Then the Dragon Master began to speak.

'We have had a lovely party . . .' he began.

'Hear! Hear!' chimed in the bigger dragons.

'And so have we,' squeaked the littlest ones.

The Dragon Master smiled. 'And now, the time has come for me to take my leave of you,' he said quietly.

There was a long, shocked silence.

'Not for ever,' the Dragon Master added gently, 'but I will be away for quite a long while. I must go to the land of fire and ice and mountains and winds, because my cousin, the Mistress of the Eastern Dragons, has asked for my help. It will be a long journey, but I will not forget you for a single moment.'

'But how will we manage without you?' asked Ember in horror.

The Dragon Master smiled and opened his arms wide. 'You will. Everything you will ever need is right here.'

'What if the Rehab comes back?'

At this, a few of the smaller dragons began to cry.

The Dragon Master gave them all a hug, one by one. 'He won't. What is there to be frightened of? You defeated him last time, all by yourselves. Anyway, I will be back as soon as I can. I promise. The Unicorn Mistress will graze her beasts on the fields nearby, and if you are in very great need, she will send her noble white stallion to gallop the clouds until he finds me.

'Now,' he said, springing to his feet and flicking his wonderful cloak back, 'I have a little game to play with you before I leave at nightfall.'

The dragons did not feel like playing games, but they listened.

'Hidden here at Kilve, there are three great treasures. They are very valuable indeed. I want you to find them, and bring them to me. When the treasures are found, I will know that you will have everything you need to look after yourselves until I return.

'Now go and get some sleep, and come back here at high tide. Then the game will begin.'

Weary and dispirited, the dragons dragged their long green tails miserably behind them, all the way back to their caves.

Everyone felt so unhappy after all the fun of the party! A few scattered to lonely places and slumped down fast asleep. Others sat sifting through their hoards, looking for their three greatest treasures.

What sort of 'treasure' did the Dragon Master want?

At high tide, they all met by a freshly built bonfire, but the dancing light and roaring heat could not cheer the cold, miserable dragons.

'Now,' said the Dragon Master, 'A clue to this game is that the treasures may not necessarily be something you can *see*.

Immediately a hubbub broke out. The older dragons wanted things that would be practical, like a cave broom or a fish drying rack. Others thought beauty was more valuable than practicality. They wanted to find the brightest pearls and the biggest corals they could.

Meanwhile, the Dragon Master was busy packing, and would give no more clues. Rows were breaking out here and there, and tempers were running high. And the Dragon Master had not even left yet!

At last, in desperation, Treasure asked Igneous to make everyone be quiet and sit down. Tired, curious and grumpy, all the dragons sat in a wide circle around the little wingless dragon. Treasure asked

Igneous if she could climb onto his back so she could see everyone.

'What do you think the Dragon Master means by "valuable treasure?" she asked, peering at the sad blue-green faces one at a time.

'Beautiful! Useful! Strong! *Edible!*' came the answers, yelled all at once by fifty different roars and squeaks.

Treasure held up a claw, and everyone fell silent. 'Let us think,' she said. 'If the Dragon Master is going away for a while, what will be the most valuable things we can have?'

There was a long silence, then, 'Good weather.'

'Plenty of fish!'

'Nothing nasty around... definitely no slugs!' came the replies. Then the arguments started again.

Fawkes said those sorts of thing didn't count, and anyway, as the treasures had to be something no one could see, the game wasn't fair.

Furnace pointed out that the Dragon Master had said that they *might* not be able to see the treasures, so good weather and no slugs *could* count. Fawkes said that was the same thing, and went into a sulk. Igneous was about to breathe some rather hot air onto Fawkes' tail when Treasure called for silence again.

'Let us all go away, calm down and *think*,' urged Treasure. 'It's probably all very simple, and right under our noses. The Dragon Master would never ask us to do the impossible!'

One by one the dragons drifted away.

Fizzle went to his cave and looked long and hard at his chocolate biscuit hoard. He knew everyone would laugh if he presented that as the greatest treasure he could find. But what else could he do? But as to the second and third treasures—that was more difficult. He would have to talk to the others about that.

Fireworks poked a claw into various bottles and powders, smiling to himself about the wonderful bangs and stinks he could make and the glorious coloured smoke rings that he could blow. Gleefully he took down his very best jar of powder. It was sky-blue-pink with purple spots. Who could doubt that *this* was the greatest treasure in Kilve? When that powder was lit the display would be glorious. It would bring happiness to everyone. But he decided to go and ask some of the others what the second and third treasures might be.

Maurice looked at his big jar of scale polish. How could life go on without that? The second treasure had to be floating on a warm thermal on a summer day, but the third one baffled him. He would ask Clarys.

Meanwhile, Clarys was deep, deep under the hills in a special place where she had hidden *her* real treasure—pieces of pretty rocks that she had collected in her cave-crawling expeditions.

Carefully she chose the biggest one she could find, a clear, white stone which caught the light with piercingly brilliant colours. If her best treasure was needed to help the dragons while their friend was away, she had to share it. If it stayed hidden in the cave, it would only be a piece of rock. Out in the sunlight, it would glisten, and maybe make one of the others feel happier. She looked about for a second and third treasure, but she could not decide. She would go and ask Sparky.

Sparky was high in the skies. Since he had learned the answer to 'why?' he had practised flying and fishing until he became the best of all the dragons. The feeling of diving out of the sky with pinpoint accuracy onto a nice fat cod was perfect joy to him. He could bring a fine fish to the meeting and perhaps tell the others about what he felt. Could that be two treasures? He'd ask Horace.

Horace looked up at the shining sun that warmed his scales. He smiled. The sun was *his* greatest treasure. He had always loved it. He filled a bucket of water, and staggered along the rocky beach to the meeting place and put it down carefully where it would catch the sun's reflection best. He sat and waited for the others, and remembered how they had flown until they were exhausted to catch the real sun for him when he was a baby. How much they cared for one another. If it wasn't such a sad day, he would be really happy.

Igneous and Furnace lay on a hilltop and puffed little golden tongues of flame up into the clear blue afternoon sky. How they loved fire! What blazes they had made! What rockfalls they had caused when they had been making new water courses under the Midnight Forest! Surely fire was the greatest gift any dragon had... but the second and third baffled them. Igneous thought it must be roast shark, until Furnace suggested it was the day they found little wingless Treasure. Why not see what she thought now?

Far in the distance they saw Treasure walking along the beach, poking at various bits of seaweed: tasting this and scratching that. Her lore of plants and weeds was great indeed, even though she was such a young dragon. At last she sighed, and turned for home. It was getting late, and she could see that some of the dragons were already making their way to the flat place where the beach met the land. There they had held their wonderful party; there they must say goodbye to their beloved Dragon Master for a long time.

As Treasure came close, she could see that all the dragons had something in their claws. There were glittery things, wriggly things, bulky things, long thin things, and tiny, secretly hidden things.

By early evening they had all arrived. It was time. The tide was high, as the clear turquoise water surged and fell, foaming against the rocks. All the dragons came and sat, still and forlorn, around their best friend.

The Dragon Master stood up. 'Well, my wise dragons, have you brought me your three most valuable treasures? Let me see if you have found what you will need for my absence.'

One by one all the dragons came up and laid their treasures on a large, flat rock. But before they went to sit down again, they each whispered something into the Dragon Master's ear.

Treasure looked at the pile of precious objects. Everything was so *different*. She was worried. There were bound to be bad arguments about which would be chosen to be the greatest treasure. Then there would be problems with sulking because various gifts *hadn't* been chosen. She wasn't looking forward to calming them down again.

She waited till last, and then presented the Dragon Master with a small pile of lava weed. 'It saved our lives once,' she said quietly. 'When we were caught by a terrible storm and stranded in the middle of the sea for *days*, we had nothing but lava weed to eat. Do you remember?'

Then she looked sad. 'But as to the second and third most valuable things . . . I'm afraid I've let you down. I'd have to talk to the others first. I couldn't possibly suggest anything until I'd heard what *they* had to say.'

Then there was silence. None of the dragons knew what to say. Who could tell what the Dragon Master would count as treasure and what was rubbish?

Looking out to sea, the Dragon Master sat quite still for a long time. Then at last he threw back his head and laughed with intense pleasure. He lifted and spread his great cloak so the stars shone and burned in the soft evening shadows. Slowly the lights grew and twinkled, reflecting on the dragons' blue-green scales and silver wings so they too shimmered with a dancing light.

The Dragon Master exclaimed: 'This is wonderful! You have all told me the same thing . . . you wanted to talk to the others before choosing. This is your first treasure: wanting to work things out together.

'Next, I have been shown the most delightful things: everything from diamonds to chocolate biscuits. It would be impossible for you all to agree on your second precious thing, because you will all see different things as important. Your 'different-ness' *is* your second treasure: being yourselves.

'Lastly, no one has laughed or teased anyone else for being different, or thought something rubbish which others see as valuable. That is your third treasure: loving each other.

'Now you have found the three great secret treasures you had hidden here, I *know* you can look after yourselves. Care for your treasures well and I will be back sooner than you think. While I am gone, fly with the West Wind!'

The Dragon Master's voice sounded funny as he finished talking. Treasure pushed her thin, cool nose into her friend's hand. 'You don't want to go, do you?' she asked softly.

The Dragon Master shook his head and sniffed. 'No, I'd much rather be here. But my cousin needs me, and more importantly, *you* need me to go for a little while. In the beginning, every time something was difficult, you dragons expected me to sort things out for you. And that was right.

'Now, you are older. If I don't go away some-times, you will never learn to fly the West Wind for yourselves. Today you have found new wings amongst your treasures. You are growing up fast, and other creatures will learn from you. There will be new adventures tomorrow, but tonight I must go ... You will be in my thoughts all the time and, when I come back, I will want to know everything you have done.'

And with that, the Dragon Master gave his beloved dragons sleep with his wonderful cloak.

Taking one last loving look at his silver-winged creatures, the Dragon Master stepped towards a white shape waiting in the shadowy edges of the Midnight Forest. Then, mounting the huge unicorn ... he was gone.

Also from Lion Publishing:

THE MAGIC IN THE POOL OF MAKING

Beth Webb

'I risked *everything* to get you that water last night. You don't realize how little we've got. There's not a drop to be spared!' Johin shouted. 'You're a Sand boy, aren't you? Your people want to steal our water. And now I've saved your life!'

The River Planet is in danger. Its life source, the Lightwater River, is dying, poisoned through centuries of pollution and misuse. Manny, a starving and mysterious Sand boy, is the only person who knows how to put things right. Now, through a simple act of kindness, Johin is entwined in his dangerous quest.

As they cross the drought-stricken land, Johin realizes that the River offers life in more than one way. But clearing its source won't be enough. She and Manny also have to defeat the evil Brilliance . . .

ISBN 0 7459 2234 1

A selection of top titles from LION PUBLISHING

THE MAGIC IN THE POOL OF MAKING	
Beth Webb	£2.99☐
TALES FROM THE ARK Avril Rowlands	£3.50☐
I SAW THREE SHIPS Elizabeth Goudge	£2.50☐
THE LITTLE WHITE HORSE Elizabeth Goudge	£2.99☐
IN THE KINGDOM OF THE CARPET DRAGON	
Ralph Batten	£1.99☐
UNDER THE GOLDEN THRONE Ralph Batten	£1.99☐
LITTLE MOCKER'S GREAT ADVENTURE	
Jean Bell Mosely	£2.50☐

All Lion paperbacks are available from your local bookshop or newsagent, or can be ordered direct from the address below. Just tick the titles you want and fill in the form.

Name (Block letters) _____

Address_____

_____

Write to Lion Publishing, Cash Sales Department, PO Box 11, Falmouth, Cornwall TR10 9EN, England.

Please enclose a cheque or postal order to the value of the cover price plus:

UK INCLUDING BFPO: £1.00 for the first book, 50p for the second book and 30p for each additional book ordered to a maximum charge of £3.00.

OVERSEAS INCLUDING EIRE: £2.00 for the first book, £1.00 for the second book and 50p for each additional book.

Lion Publishing reserves the right to show on covers and charge new retail prices which may differ from those previously advertised in the text or elsewhere, and to increase postal rates in accordance with the Post Office.